Life after Wife

AMBER KELLY

Cover Design: Sommer Stein, Perfect Pear Creative Covers
Cover Image: Regina Wamba
Editor: Jovana Shirley, Unforeseen Editing, www.unforeseenediting.com
Proofreader: Judy Zweifel, Judy's Proofreading
Formatter: Champagne Book Design

To Erin and Jena.
You two have shown us all how beautiful life after wife can be.
Here's to the next thirty years of friendship.

Life after Wife

prologue

Taeli
Seventeen Years Ago

I START SNATCHING MY CLOTHES FROM THE CLOSET, FLINGING THEM inside the suitcase on my bed, when a soft knock sounds on my bedroom door.

"Taeli, sweetheart, can I come in?" Daddy asks.

I swipe at the tears on my cheeks and walk over to unlock and open the door.

His eyes land on the suitcase, and he sighs.

"You're really leaving?" he asks.

I nod. "Damon is on his way to pick me up. We're flying to Chicago in the morning."

"I wish you'd wait until the end of the summer."

"Why? So Mom can spend the next thirty days telling me what a disappointment I am?"

"She didn't mean any of that. She's just angry," he says.

"It sure sounded like she meant it. I'm sorry I'm not the perfect daughter, but this is my life."

"Your mother doesn't want to see you throw away the opportunities you've been given or see your talents go to waste. We're not saying to break up with the boy. We're just asking you to wait. Give it another year and see how you feel then."

"I don't want to wait a year. He was accepted into Northwestern, and I'm going with him."

"Are you sure this is what you want?" he asks.

"I love him, Daddy."

He sits down on the foot of my bed and pats the spot beside him. I sit and lay my head on his shoulder.

"Love, huh? I know better than to argue with a woman in love. I guess that settles it."

"It does for me. He makes me happy. Why can't Mom be happy for me?"

"You and your mother are more alike than you realize, kiddo. You're both lead by your heart. That's why you two butt heads so often."

"Alike? More like complete opposites," I disagree.

He chuckles.

"You're both hard-headed as well."

I shrug.

"Maybe a little."

"Promise me one thing, Taeli. Someday, you're gonna want to come home, but your pride is going to get in the way, and you're gonna think it's too late. When that happens, you come home anyway because it'll never be too late."

"I promise."

Chapter one

I GLANCE INTO THE REARVIEW MIRROR TO SEE THAT MY TWELVE-YEAR-old son is still laser-focused on the tablet in his hand. He has had his earbuds in and a game in progress since we crossed the Illinois state line, headed for my home state of Tennessee. That's approximately eight hours and nearly five hundred seventy miles without one word from him other than to ask for a bathroom break and a Gatorade.

I know that picking up our lives and moving to my hometown of Balsam Ridge wasn't exactly on his agenda for the summer. He planned to attend a soccer camp with his best friends to hone his skills for next year's middle school tryouts. He wanted to swim at the community pool with our neighbors. He expected it to be a normal school break, like all the ones that had come before.

Yeah, well, so did I, kid.

I was supposed to head up the neighborhood's Fourth of July planning committee. I intended to start tennis lessons at the club to improve my serve. I wanted to have mimosa brunches with friends and to take a family vacation to Cabo.

Never in my wildest dreams did I fathom returning to the small mountain town where I had grown up, but when the twenty-four-year-old medical assistant to your husband of sixteen years knocks on your door one rainy Thursday afternoon to inform you that she is pregnant with his child, you tend to do unfathomable things.

Damon is an internal medicine physician in private practice in Chicago. We met at the University of Tennessee during my freshman year. He was a senior and had been accepted into the medical school program at Northwestern. After a brief but passionate courtship, I fell madly in love and decided to drop out of school, leaving my full-ride athletic scholarship behind and following him to Chicago. We married the following spring. He went on to medical school, and I went to work as an office administrator for a machine tool manufacturing firm. I also worked nights to support us, making collection calls for a cellular company, while Damon spent his time, including nights and weekends, studying and doing his clinical rotations.

We were busy humans, ships passing in the night but bumping into one another enough to create another tiny human and drag him into the chaotic fray.

Caleb was born between Damon's graduation from medical school and his first year of residency. It wasn't easy—juggling my two jobs, the residency, and parenthood—but we made it work. It was a delicate balance that got a little easier once Damon finished his residency, and with the financial backing of his parents and a substantial business loan, we opened Lowder Family Medicine in Naperville.

I brought my office manager skills to the family business, and Damon was the talent. Caleb was four years old when the practice opened, and he spent many hours entertaining himself under the desk on my office floor while I worked.

By the time Caleb started third grade and had a dozen

commitments, including baseball and soccer practices and games, the business was out of the red, and we decided to hire an administrative manager so that I could be a stay-at-home mom. My reward for all the years of sacrifice.

It was glorious. I had worked so hard, for so long so that Damon could open his own practice, and all that work was finally paying off. We built our dream home in our dream neighborhood. I made mom friends through PTA and at the community pool. We joined the local country club, and I became a lady who lunched with other ladies while our husbands were at work and our kids were at school. My job became keeping a magazine spread–worthy home, being a social director for an eight-year-old, playing tennis, practicing yoga, going to Botox parties, and keeping myself in top physical shape for my husband. I was damn good at it too.

At the time, when Caleb started middle school, we had a seamless routine, living in our happy suburban bubble. At least, I thought so. I was living with blinders on. I stopped going to the office for noonday kisses and to say hello to the staff. I stopped paying attention to who was hired and fired. I no longer questioned Damon's extra-long hours at the office and when he stopped taking half-days off on Fridays. I wasn't alarmed at the number of after-hours emergencies that had to be handled in the middle of the night. I got comfortable and became numb to it all.

I was living in a beautiful house of cards until that twenty-four-year-old with her cheap hair extensions and enhanced figure kicked it over one hot, humid May afternoon, and it all came tumbling down.

Damon didn't even try to deny it. I called his cell while she was still standing at my front door and screamed the allegations at him. He politely asked if we could discuss the "issue" when he got home.

The issue? Really?

Ivy, the homewrecker, was as composed and confident as could be when she blew my bubble apart. She was non-apologetic as she professed her love for my husband and explained her intention to keep his love child.

Love.

As if either of them knew what that word meant.

I shut the door in the tramp's face, went upstairs, and packed a bag for me and a bag for Caleb. I picked him up from school. I checked us into a deluxe suite at The Peninsula Chicago, using Damon's black card, and I turned off my cell phone.

It took him two days to track us down and another two days to talk me into returning home. His mother was there to watch Caleb while we discussed things, but I was fairly sure he'd called her to be a referee or a witness should I stab him in the neck.

I tried to stay calm. I kept telling myself that Damon loved me and it all had to be a misunderstanding. Ivy was probably some tart who was looking for a windfall. A simple paternity test would clear up this entire matter.

By the time my mother-in-law had rounded Caleb up in her car to take him for pizza, I was as cool as a cucumber. Damon poured us a glass of wine, and we sat down in the living room on the exquisite Ambella sofa that I had special-ordered in Venetian ivory, which had just been delivered the week before. I'd planned and invited all our friends to a dinner party the following weekend to show off the new statement piece of furniture. That was before my husband's playmate visited me.

"I'm glad you came back."

"Tell me it isn't true. That you didn't throw away sixteen years of marriage for a romp with your assistant. Tell me she made it all up and you'll fire her and we can go on with our lives."

"I, um ..."

"Oh my God, Damon. You didn't!"

"I didn't mean for it to happen. It was an accident."

I carefully set my wineglass down on the coaster and slapped him as hard as I could across his cheek.

"You cheating asshole," I screeched.

He grabbed my hand before I reared back again.

"Stop it. You're being ridiculous."

"I'm being ridiculous? How do you accidentally sleep with another woman? Did you trip in the office after an emergency call, fall on top of her, and your penis slipped out of your scrubs and into her vagina?"

"Of course not. I messed up. I made a mistake."

"A mistake. Oh, silly me. A mistake. That's no big deal. Except for the oopsie you left behind in her uterus."

He sighed, and his head fell into his hands. "She said she was protected."

"And you believed her? You're a doctor, for fuck's sake. How many times have you told a young man to make sure he protects himself?"

"I know. It was stupid. But you do stupid things when you're in love."

"Love?!"

He brought his eyes to mine.

"I thought it was an accident, a mistake?"

"It was. I didn't mean to fall for someone else."

I stood and started walking back toward the kitchen island. All of a sudden, I was dizzy, and I felt like I might throw up. I was angry at his indiscretion. I expected him to deny it or cry and beg for forgiveness—not profess his love for another woman.

He stood and reached for me, and I swatted at his hands.

Pain slid down my spine as reality sunk in.

"Get out!" I cried.

"Taeli."

"I said, get out!" I screamed.

"We have to talk about this."

"No. I don't feel like talking. I want you to leave."

He raised his hands in surrender. "That's fine. I'll go. For now."

A horn blows from the car behind me and shakes me from my memory. I give him a curt wave and gun it through the traffic light that apparently turned green while I was reminiscing.

"Mom!"

Caleb's irritated voice comes from the backseat, and I look in the mirror to see him scowling at me.

"Sorry, buddy."

"Are we close?" he asks.

I nod toward the sign up ahead that reads, *Welcome to Balsam Ridge. One thousand two hundred fifty-seven smiling faces and one old grump.*

His eyes skim the road sign.

"Is there really an old grump?" he asks.

"Oh, yeah, and you'll know when you meet him," I answer, hoping to get a smile or a grin or even a grunt from him.

He just rolls his eyes and looks back down at his monitor.

Needless to say, I'm not winning any Mom of the Year prizes anytime soon. My kid hates me. Not his father. Me.

I don't blame him. I'm the one who ripped him from his home and everyone he knew and fled to the hills once word got out about Damon and Ivy.

You see, in Naperville, it's all about who you know and what you have. Girlfriends might have your back at brunch when you complain about your husband, but it's a different story when shit really and truly hits the fan. And Dr. Damon Lowder is more important to remain friends with than his cheated-on and dumped wife. Shunned. That's me. Poor, pitiful, shunned Taeli. I had to escape. Damon can have our ex–dream home, our ex-friends, and our ex-life. To hell with them all.

So, here we are, ten miles from my mother's house. The home where my brother, Gene, and I grew up. The place I couldn't wait to leave in the rearview mirror the second I graduated high school.

Fuck me.

The sun starts its descent behind the mountain as we turn onto the gravel road that winds up to the old farmhouse.

The road is narrow, the climb is steep, and there's not a streetlight or guardrail in sight.

I throw the Volvo XC90 into four-wheel drive, and rocks ricochet off the tires and ping against the undercarriage.

Caleb removes his earbuds and tosses his tablet across the seat.

"What's wrong, buddy?" I ask.

"There's no reception," he says as he looks out the window and his eyes go wide.

"Pretty, isn't it?" I ask as he takes in the view.

"We're going to fall down the mountain," he says with a tremor in his voice.

"No, we aren't. Your momma can drive these mountain roads with her eyes closed. This is my old stomping ground. I learned how to drive a stick on this very gravel."

"A stick?"

"Yep, a manual stick shift truck with no automatic steering. It was a beast. My daddy made me stop and start every half-mile straight up the mountain. I wore the clutch out on that old truck, but by the time I had to go take my driver's test, I could drive it as well as he could," I say with pride.

"Good job," he says, sarcastically raising his thumbs in the air.

This sweet child of mine.

We finally make it to the top at fifty-two hundred feet and turn into the open gate. I park in front of the house.

It looks the same as it did the day I left. A two-story robin's-egg-blue Colonial farmhouse with white trim. A wide-columned front porch with a large bay window from the dining room that overlooks the yard. Gone is the shingled roof from my childhood, and in its place is soft gray tin.

I take a deep breath as I turn off the ignition.

I haven't been back here since my father's funeral five years ago. I half-expected the place to be a dilapidated ruin, not the postcard picture–worthy scene before me.

"You ready, buddy?" I ask as I glance back at Caleb.

"I guess," he mumbles as he gathers his things.

We exit the vehicle as my mother, Leona Tilson, appears on the front porch, her face alight.

She is a sight in her long green kaftan. Her silver hair is held back from her face with a headband. I can hear her booming voice before a word leaves her mouth as she stretches out her arms.

Here goes nothing.

Chapter
two

Taeli

"MY BABIES," SHE CALLS.

Caleb runs up the steps ahead of me, still clutching his tablet, and Mom envelops him in a tight hug and holds on until he is squirming.

"I can't breathe, Granna," he mumbles against her bosom.

She laughs and releases him. Then, she puts her fists on her hips and looks him up and down.

"I swear you have grown twice your size since I saw you last. You're going to be a giant. Have you been eating magic beans?" she asks.

He giggles.

"What?"

"The giant doesn't eat the magic beans, Mom. Jack plants them, so he can climb the giant beanstalk," I interrupt.

Her eyes come to me. "Are you sure?" she asks.

"Positive."

Needless to say, Mom was not the one reading Gene and me bed-time stories at night. Daddy handled that job.

"I like my version better," she says before looking back down at Caleb. "Go grab your things, and I'll show you to your room. Dinner is almost ready."

Caleb hands her his tablet and trots back down the steps to the SUV. I click the button on the key fob, and the back hatch releases, so he can start unloading his bags.

"Thanks for letting us stay the summer, Mom," I say as we both watch him.

"Of course." She waves me off.

"It'll be temporary. I just need to get my head together and figure out our next move before the school year starts," I promise.

"Don't rush yourself, kiddo. This is your home too. Take as long as you need. Besides, I'm looking forward to having my grandson for an entire summer," she assures me.

I shake my head.

This hasn't been my home in a very long time. Truth be told, I'm not sure where home is anymore, but I have to find it. For Caleb's sake.

"Well, I'll get my things," I say before descending the steps.

There is so much to say, but neither of us has ever been good at communicating. Daddy was always the buffer between the two of us, and now that he is gone, us living under the same roof should be in-teresting. Hopefully, we won't want to kill each other.

Thank goodness for Caleb.

"Here you are. This used to be your uncle Gene's room," Mom says as she leads us into the spare bedroom.

Caleb tosses his suitcase on the bed and looks around the space.

My brother lived here with my parents and helped run the old farm until our father died. He upped and took off to New Orleans with an older woman two days after we laid Daddy to rest. Although you'd never guess he left from the looks of this room. His dusty boots are still sitting beside the desk in the far corner. His coat is hanging on the back of the closet door. There is still a pile of junk and coins on the bedside table, as if he had just emptied his pockets the night before.

"I cleaned you out a spot in the closet to hang some things, and you have the top two drawers in the chest. If you need more room, just shove your uncle's stuff aside. The computer is old, but it works fine if you need it." Mom chatters away.

"It's fine, Granna. I didn't bring much," Caleb assures her.

"Do you remember where the bathroom is?" she asks.

He nods. "At the end of the hallway."

"Why don't you run and wash up for dinner while I get your mom settled?"

We follow him out, and Mom opens the door on the other side of the hall that leads to my old bedroom.

"I had a friend help me bring the twin bed from the attic down for you," she says as I walk inside.

The room is much smaller than I remember. It still has the same lilac walls and beige carpet that it did when I moved out to attend UT, but my bed is gone, as is the rest of my furniture. It was replaced with Mom's sewing table and craft armoire, which has been moved against the far wall to make room for the tiny bed.

She walks over to the closet and opens the door. She shoves the dress mannequins to the side.

"There you go. Plenty of space. We'll fetch a chest of drawers down from storage for you as well."

I take a seat on the end of the bed.

"This is good, Mom. I'm just here to catch my breath. There is no need to drag furniture around."

She joins me on the bed.

"You don't know how to be still. You never have. Always running a hundred miles an hour since the day you took your first step."

She places her hand on top of mine. "I know you're lost right now, kiddo, but you'll find your way. I promise. And home is always a good place to start."

There is a knock at the door downstairs, and Caleb yells that he'll get it as he emerges from the bathroom.

Mom and I follow him and make it down the stairs just as he opens the door and is greeted by a deep voice.

"Hi there."

"Hi. Who are you?" Caleb asks.

"I'm Graham. And you are?"

"I'm Caleb Lowder."

"It's nice to meet you, Caleb."

Mom joins them in the foyer.

"Graham, come in. I'd like you to meet my daughter," Mom says.

He steps through the threshold, and I have to grab hold of the railing to keep myself from fleeing up the steps.

Graham Tuttle. What is he doing here?

"Taeli, this is Graham. He's my friend Sara-Beth's boy. He and his brothers help me around here from time to time. He brought the bed down for you," Mom introduces us.

He smiles up at me.

"I know you," I blurt out.

"You do?" he asks. His brow furrows as he tries to place me.

I gather my wits and walk the few steps down and extend my hand. "Sort of. I went to school with your brothers."

He takes my offered hand into his. "Which ones?" he asks.

"Garrett and Corbin and Weston was a grade behind me. I knew all of them, except for you and Langford. I knew of you of course, but you guys were older," I babble, as if he doesn't know how old he is.

Every girl in the county carried a crush on one or more of the Tuttle brothers.

He grins, and his jade eyes dance with amusement.

Great.

Mom clears her throat.

"I was just about to serve dinner. Would you like to join us?" she asks.

He turns to her. My hand is still in his.

"I wish I could, but I have to get back to the office. I was just delivering the concrete pad for your new generator. The boys will be by in the morning to set it up and do all the wiring for you. You're going to like this one. It has a remote, so all you have to do is push a button. No more going out to the breaker box in the middle of a storm."

She claps her hands. "Oh, thank you, Jesus." She looks at me. "Graham here is making me a modern woman. He even installed a tankless hot water heater and an irrigation system that works on a timer. I don't have to go out with a hose and water the garden anymore."

He turns his attention back to me. "The last big downpour we had, she slipped in the mud and sprained her ankle trying to get the generator started. She sat out there in the pouring rain for an hour before she was able to get up to the porch," he informs me.

"What?"

"Oh, it wasn't as bad as it sounds," Mom insists.

"It could have been worse," Graham points out.

"You're just a worrywart," Mom teases.

"And you're a stubborn woman," he tosses back at her.

She laughs.

Graham realizes he still has ahold of my hand, and he releases me.

"I'd best be going. It was nice to meet you, Taeli, and you too, Caleb. Leona, I'll be back tomorrow afternoon to check on the work and make sure everything is up and running for you," he says.

He kisses my mother on her cheek, and then he walks out the door.

I watch as he makes his way to a black truck with the words *Tuttle Contracting* on the side panel.

Mom comes up beside me. "That boy is a godsend," she mutters.

"Is he?" I ask.

"Oh, yes, he helps me a lot around here. He's a handsome devil too. I just can't understand why some woman hasn't snatched him up yet," she says and then turns to Caleb. "Who's hungry?"

"Me!" Caleb exclaims.

"Come along, then. Let's set the table."

They trot off in the direction of the kitchen. I walk out on the porch and watch the truck disappear down the drive.

Graham Tuttle is one of the infamous sons of the Tuttle family dynasty. Okay, maybe that's a little too dramatic, but the Tuttles are considered Balsam Ridge royalty. His parents, Hilton and Sara-Beth, inherited a lion's share of property and businesses in town. His great-grandfather outright owned two of the surrounding mountains and the valley itself in the late 1800s long before it became the tourist destination it now is.

In the 1930s, sometime after the Great Depression, his great-grandfather and his grandfather formed Tuttle and Son Realty, and they began to section off and sell acreage on the mountain. My grandparents purchased twenty acres from them and started the farm that my mother still lives on today.

When Graham's father, Hilton, came along, they started Tuttle Contracting, and that's when the valley itself came to be.

The valley runs alongside the Coyote River bank, which made it the perfect place to start catering to visitors in the summer. Motels and inns popped up every quarter of a mile, as did several churches. Mom-and-pop restaurants and independent boutiques lined Market Square, along with ice cream shops, coffee shops, and watering holes.

Then, the gem mines, campgrounds, mini-golf, arcades, souvenir shops, festival grounds, crafters, potters, woodworkers, furniture makers, and fishing supply shops came next. However, you'll never find a franchise in the town limits. If you want a Big Mac, Starbucks latte, Walmart, or a mall, you'll have to drive at least forty minutes toward Knoxville to find them.

By the time I started school, Hilton Tuttle had married Sara-Beth, and they had six boys of their own. He changed the name to Tuttle and Sons Realty, and together, he and his wife began to build cabins and cottages all along the river and up on the mountainside and opened Rocky Pass Vacation Rentals. They also contributed a substantial amount of money to open the Balsam Ridge Golf and Country Club.

Today, the valley thrives with tens of thousands of hikers, campers, tubers, fishermen, and other nature enthusiasts visiting every spring and summer. Fall vacationers come to see the autumn foliage when the mountains turn a vivid rainbow of yellow, orange, and red, and now, with the imminent opening of the Balsam Ridge Ski Area and Coyote Mountain Snow Tubing, the town is going to be a year-round place of adventure. All of which was made possible by the Tuttle family.

However, you'd never be able to pick them out of a crowd. With the exception of Garrett Tuttle, who is a talented musician who ran off to Nashville after he graduated, the family is as down-to-earth as any other resident of Balsam Ridge. They work with their hands, and they participate in the community. Sara-Beth was my Sunday school teacher, and Hilton coached my middle school volleyball team. They didn't parade around in fancy cars, wearing fur coats and pearls, and wave to the townsfolk like we were their minions or the dirt beneath their feet. When we were children, we never would have guessed that Langford, Graham, Garrett, Corbin, Weston, or Morris was any better off than the rest of us. They were just those Tuttle boys.

Tuttle men now.

Chapter three

Graham

I WALK INTO MY PARENTS' HOUSE AND FIND MOM AT THE STOVE, preparing scrambled eggs. I kiss her cheek and take a seat at the island.

"Good morning, sweetheart. What brings you out this way?" she asks.

"I'm looking for Pop. I have a little time before I need to be out at Leona's and thought we could ride out to the campground and take a look at the pool."

She finishes and turns off the burner. She reaches into the cupboard above the microwave and retrieves three plates and sets them on the island.

"I can't believe it's leaking again already. You guys just replaced the liner last spring," she says as she scoops the eggs on the plate.

"I know. It's the weather. It's been stormier than usual, and with all the trees out there, every time the wind blows, limbs end up in the pool. I think that's how it keeps getting punctured."

She loads the plates with bacon she had resting in the microwave and biscuits from the oven. Then, she pushes one of them in front of me.

That's Mom. She had no idea I was coming over this morning, but after raising six sons, she knows to always make extra. I don't think the woman could cook for just the two of them if she tried.

"What's the solution, then? I hate to remove trees. They give good shade, and I think the campers like the feeling of being in the woods," she asks.

I agree. The last thing I'd ever want to do is cut down trees if there is another way.

"I have a few ideas. I'm sure we can save the trees."

"Thank goodness. Your father was ready to take a chainsaw to them yesterday," she tells me.

"Are you talking about me again?" Pop asks as he comes into the kitchen and heads to the coffeemaker, pouring himself a mug.

She smiles up at him. "I sure am."

He kisses her on the lips and smacks her behind, causing her to jump before he joins me at the bar to eat his breakfast.

"So, what are you thinking, son?" he asks as he salts and peppers his eggs.

"I think it's time to consider converting it to concrete," I suggest.

We've had this conversation before. Dad has always been opposed because of the time and cost it'd take to do the conversion. He doesn't want to inconvenience his longtime renters with the construction mess, nor does he like the idea of having the pool unusable for several months because it is one of the amenities his guests look forward to enjoying.

The campground is an eighteen-acre resort that offers two hundred and fifty full-hookup gravel and grass sites for RVs, fifteen tiny chalets along the creek for weekly rental, a bathhouse, laundry, motorcycle shelters, fenced dog park, pool, and community pavilion with gas grills, a firepit, and a playground.

Many of the campers keep their RVs there year-round and have rented their sites for generations. They spend most weekends through the summer and a majority of their holidays in our valley. Mom and Pop consider them family. They have watched their kids grow up and have kids of their own.

Pop sighs. "I know you're right. I was hoping this latest liner would last through the end of the summer. I hate for the children not to have the pool to play in."

"That's why I dropped by. Let's go take a look at the tear. If it's in a place where it can be patched, I'll get one of my guys out there to drain it tonight and get it repaired. That way, it'll be down two days, tops, to dry and then refill. We can have it open by the weekend. If we're lucky, it will hold at least a couple of months. Then, we can close it for the season and start the construction. It will give us plenty of time to convert over the winter."

He slides his eyes to me. He knows as well as I do that the winter months here in Balsam Ridge are unpredictable. We could be covered in snow from December to March, making construction projects complicated.

"That will make the pavilion area a construction zone, and people won't be able to have bonfires or enjoy roasting hot dogs or making s'mores by the firepit," he grumbles.

"He means, *he* won't get to enjoy the s'mores and hot dogs everyone makes," Mom teases.

"We can put up temporary walls and tents around the area. I think we can block off the firepit area and just sacrifice the pool and the stage. I know it sucks, but they will love the new pool. My guys can put in a tanning ledge for the moms to sunbathe on while their kids splash around. I'll do a pebble finish, so it's not rough on their feet, and if a pup jumps in, their claws won't do any damage."

Dogs are not allowed in the pool. They have their own splash pads in the dog park, but an occasional pet goes rogue and ends up taking a swim, and of course, we have our friendly neighborhood critters to contend with.

"All right, let's see if it can be patched, and we'll close it a tad earlier this year, so you can start in September. That way, you can beat the bad weather." He gives in.

"Great. Let's go," I say as I stand.

"Can I finish my breakfast first?" he asks.

I look at my watch. "If you hurry. I have a crew at Leona's, installing a generator, and I promised her I'd be by at lunch to inspect the work and teach her how it works."

Mom takes my plate to the sink and refills my coffee cup.

"You know, Leona's daughter and grandson are in town," she says.

"Yeah, I met them yesterday," I tell her.

She leans over the island. "Isn't Taeli lovely? Leona shows me pictures of her and Caleb all the time. It's just awful, what she's been through. Leona is tickled that she finally left that no-good husband of hers."

I shrug. "I guess. I only saw them for a minute."

"Maybe when you're out there this afternoon, you can chat. You know, make her feel welcome. I'm sure it's hard, coming home after all these years," she suggests.

I give her a stern look. "Mom," I say.

"I'm just saying, she could use a friend."

Pop chuckles, and she snaps her eyes to him.

"You're as subtle as a brick through a window," he states.

She tosses a potholder at his head. Then, her attention comes back to me.

"It wouldn't hurt you to be nice to her," she declares.

"I'm nice to everyone, Mom. I'll be nice to Taeli and her kid too."

"That's all I'm asking."

Pop's eyes slide to me. We both know that she is infamous for meddling. As a mother to six rebellious and rambunctious sons, she has a knack for orchestrating meet-cutes with women she deems worthy of her boys. In fact, she is the one who introduced me to my wife.

Heather was the daughter of one of the ladies in Mom's prayer group at church. Mom hired her to run the front desk at the campground the same summer she hired me to be the on-site manager. She knew if she just put the two of us in the same orbit, we'd fall madly in love and live happily ever after. And she was right. Before the summer was over, I was one hundred percent smitten with the shy beauty. The next summer, I put a ring on her finger.

We were blissfully happy for four glorious years before a diagnosis blew our bubble apart. Stage four breast cancer. Then, we had two terrifying and painful years before I laid her to rest up on the mountain beside my grandmother and grandfather.

That was eleven years ago this past May.

It took me several years before I could even ask someone to dinner. As the years have passed, it's gotten easier, but I've never had a relationship that lasted more than a few months before it fizzled out. Not because I refuse to give my heart to another woman—Heather wouldn't have wanted me to grieve forever—but because I just haven't run across anyone who makes my heart skip the way she did. Once you've had that kind of spark with another human, you know when it's missing with someone else.

"I'm serious," Mom insists.

"Taeli and Leona haven't had the best relationship since she moved away, and she is hoping that this time together will give them a chance to mend fences. With her beloved husband, Bernard, passing away suddenly, and Gene running off, this will be good for her. She's my friend, and I want this for her. So, if that means each of us makes an effort to help Taeli and her son acclimate into the community, then that's what we will do," she commands.

We all love Leona. She and Mom are very close, and my brothers and I treat her like a second mother. One or more of us are at her home almost daily, taking care of things she needs done around the farm or being fed until we have to roll back down the mountain. She's a funny, lovable, and quirky woman, and we all get a kick out of spending time with her.

"I promise to try and make them feel exceptionally welcome," I assure her.

Her eyes brighten. "Thank you."

Once Pop and I take a look at the damage, we conclude the patch will work for now and set to start draining the pool. Some of the kids look on in despair as Pop hangs the Closed sign on the entry gate, so he takes my truck and runs to the hardware store to buy a dozen inflatable pools and several water sprinklers to attach to hoses and run through the grassy area beside the playground.

When he returns and sets everything up, he decides to stay and hang out with the families while I take off to Leona's. As I pull out of the site, an ice cream truck pulls in. I look in the rearview mirror and see Pop hand the man a wad of cash as all the kids stand around his feet, waiting for their treats.

He's a sucker for those tiny humans.

I make my way up the mountain and arrive just as my crew is loading up the van with their tools.

"Hey, boss," John says as I park.

"How did it go?" I ask as I exit and meet them in the driveway.

"It should be up and running. We reworked the electrical box and added a kill switch that will turn off the entire breaker, and we wired the generator straight to the box. That way, she can flip one switch to shut off the entire box and then hit the button on this remote to start the generator up. Once power is restored, all she has to do is turn off the generator and flip the box back on," he explains.

"Thanks. That will be a lot easier for her. Are you guys heading out to lunch?"

"Yeah, Brian is filling the generator with gasoline now, and I stored an extra tank in the barn," he says.

"Lunch is on me today. Use your company card to pay for it," I say.

"Thanks, boss. See you back at the shop," he says as he hands the remote off to me.

I go in search of Leona to teach her how to work everything. I walk around the back of the house and pass Brian as he makes his way to the van. I inspect the work, and it looks great. The equipment fits nicely on the concrete pad, and the guys extended the overhang, which shelters the heating and air units to protect them from snow and ice, to cover the generator as well.

Leona emerges onto the back deck and calls to me.

"Graham, it looks good, doesn't it?" she says, pleased with the job.

"It does. If you have a minute, I'll show you how it works."

She descends the new steps with a guardrail my brothers Weston and Morris installed last week to make it safer for her to walk down to the breaker box during a storm.

I show her the new kill switch and how to operate the remote control. She is thrilled with the setup.

"I feel so high-tech," she declares.

Leona Tilson is an easy woman to please.

"I'm glad you like it. I'll definitely make life a bit simpler for you this winter."

"Thank you, Graham. Come on in for a glass of lemonade," she requests.

"It is lunchtime," I say as I follow her inside.

"Perfect timing. I just took a chicken casserole out of the oven," she calls over her shoulder.

"My favorite," I tell her, which is something she already knows.

Chapter
four

Taeli

I T IS JARRING, WAKING UP IN MY OLD ROOM. AS I OPEN MY EYES, I have to blink a couple of extra times until the walls come into focus and I realize where I am.

I throw the covers over my head to escape the sunlight peeking in the window from between the cream lace curtains. I forgot how much brighter mountain mornings are.

I hide for as long as I can, ignoring the sounds of Mom puttering around the kitchen. When the banging underneath the window of my room begins, I know it's time I get up and face the day.

Settling for only a cup of coffee in lieu of the chocolate chip pancake breakfast Mom and Caleb enjoy, I decide to take a long, hot bath before I get ready for the day.

I do my best thinking in the bathtub—always have. It's like the warm water lulls my sore, stressed-out body into a calmness that allows my mind to tackle the big issues and think through what my next steps will be. It might sound nuts to others, but moms understand.

The bathroom is the only place of true privacy. It's a sanctuary from our demanding families.

While I soak, I devise a plan for the day. My goal is to get Caleb out into the fresh air and give him a tour of the place where I grew up. This might not be the summer he had in mind, but I'm going to do everything in my power to make it a great one. For him and for me. Balsam Ridge is a far cry from the city, but it holds it's own unique charm, especially for children. Growing up here was magical and I have often wished Caleb had the same small-town adventures to enjoy. This is my chance to introduce him to the fun of nature.

After about an hour of me time, I get out and throw on a strapless mint-green sundress and run a brush through my hair. I skip makeup and settle for moisturizer and lip balm. Then, I make my way back downstairs to find my son.

When I make it to the hallway at the bottom of the steps, I pause in front of the collage of photos Mom has hanging above a wooden bench.

I run my fingers across the frame of a picture of me and my daddy sitting on the back of his old truck. The one of Gene pushing me on the old tire swing makes me laugh. I have such a look of terror on my face. He would push me so hard that I would swear I was about to fly up to the roof of the house. Then, there is one of me in my volleyball uniform. I'm in the air above my teammates, spiking a ball over the net. It was the state championship game my senior year. I was named MVP afterward, and it was one of my proudest moments.

I hear footsteps coming up the hall and stopping behind me.

"Is that you?" a deep voice asks, and I startle.

I was expecting Mom, but I turn quickly to find Graham Tuttle looking over my shoulder.

Where did he come from?

He looks down at me. "I'm sorry. I didn't mean to scare you," he apologizes.

"It's okay," I tell him, and he smiles and nods toward the photo on the wall. "Yes, that's me. The last game of my senior year."

"It's a good picture," he muses.

I sigh. "Yeah, I wish I still had that lean athlete's figure," I admit.

"Why?" he asks.

I turn to face him.

Isn't it obvious?

"Because I couldn't squeeze a leg into those uniform shorts now," I state.

His eyes move from my face down, taking in my dress, and back up.

"Soft curves that fill out a dress like that are nothing to wish away," he says, and my knees turn to jelly. "Don't go wishing them away."

Oh my.

We are locked in a heated staredown when Mom's head pops around the corner.

"Come on, you two. Lunch is on the table," she announces before disappearing into the kitchen again.

"After you," Graham says, stepping to the side so I can walk past him.

Caleb is seated at the table, and Mom is scooping a helping of chicken casserole on his plate. I take the seat beside him, and Graham sits across from us.

Mom tells us to help ourselves, and we load our plates while she fetches a pitcher of fresh squeezed lemonade from the fridge.

Once we all dig in, Mom asks what the plan is for today.

"I thought I'd take Caleb and show him around town. Let him see his mom's old stomping grounds," I tell them.

"That sounds like fun, doesn't it, Caleb?" she asks.

He just shrugs as he shovels food into his mouth.

"There are a few new attractions you guys should check out. We have our own vineyard now. What's it called, Graham?" Mom asks.

"Shining Rock Winery," he answers.

"That's right—Shining Rock. They have really good wines, and they have a café that makes an excellent fig and pear salad. They even bottle grape juice for the kiddos to enjoy."

"Where is it?" I ask.

"You know, I can't remember. I'm so bad with directions. Maybe you could show them, Graham," she suggests.

He stops with a forkful of chicken casserole in midair. His eyes slide to Mom.

I want to crawl under the table.

"We wouldn't want to impose. I'm sure I'll be able to find it. Besides, Caleb would probably enjoy riding the trolley through the valley more than a winery," I quickly interject.

Mom shrugs. "I just know that you enjoy wine and thought it would be fun."

"I have to get back to work," Graham begins.

"See, he has to work," I quip.

"But," he continues, "I'll be happy to show you another time. Maybe this weekend, if you don't have other plans."

"That would be lovely. Wouldn't it, Taeli?" Mom answers for me.

"I guess," I say, not wanting to be rude.

"It's a date, then," Mom decides.

"Not a date," Graham and I say in unison.

"Oh, relax. I didn't mean a *date*, date."

I give her a look that says, *Stop.*

I finish my lunch in silence as Graham and Caleb chat about school and the missed soccer camp.

I'm in awe of how easily he gets my closed-off son to open up. Caleb is not a talker. He's more the grunt-and-mumble type. I have to pry information out of him, yet here he is, animatedly chatting with a man he's known all of twenty-four hours.

Do all kids hate the sound of their mother's voice or just mine?

"Mom?"

Caleb's call pulls me from my thoughts.

"Yes?" I ask.

"Can I go?" he asks impatiently.

"I'm sorry, bud. I wasn't listening. Can you go where?"

He huffs. "To the campground with Graham."

"Now?" I ask, confused.

"Graham was just telling us that he left his father at the campground, entertaining the children with water guns and sprinklers. He thought Caleb might enjoy dropping by and meeting some of the kids his age and cooling off in the water," Mom explains.

"What about the trolley?" I ask Caleb.

"Can we do that another day?" he asks.

"I guess so," I mutter, disappointed.

"I didn't mean to cut into your plans. I'm going to be working out there all day, and I'm sure Dad and the kids will be playing into the evening. Then, we'll probably fire up the grills and throw some hot dogs on them. You two should stop by," Graham says to me and then turns back to Caleb. "After your day of exploring with your mom."

Caleb frowns, but he doesn't object.

Then, all their eyes look to me for an answer.

"We can do that," I agree.

"Then, it's settled," Mom gleefully announces.

After lunch, Graham says his good-byes, and Caleb and I help Mom with the dishes.

"Do you want to come with us today, Granna?" Caleb asks.

"Oh, no. You and your mother need some alone time," she tells him.

"No, we don't. All we ever are is alone," he tells her. "Dad moved out, and all Mom wants to do is hide in her pajamas and watch TV all day."

"I do not," I object.

His head turns to me.

"Uh huh. You haven't wanted to go anywhere since Dad left. You barely even shower."

He's right. I spent the better part of the last few months of the school year avoiding people. I knew the state of my marriage and Damon's new lover were the topics of conversations in all the school drop-off and pickup lines and every end-of-year PTA function. The last thing I wanted to do was pretend that everything was fine. That I was okay. I just couldn't stomach the whispers and the looks of pity from my former friends. So, I hid, and Caleb was the one who suffered the most.

"Well, that's all about to change. No more mopey mom for you," I promise him.

He just rolls his eyes.

"You're welcome to come with us, Mom," I offer.

She waves me off. "No, no. I have a busy afternoon planned myself. I'm getting my yoga room together," she says.

"Your what?"

"My yoga room. I've been seeing a masseuse down at The Root Cellar Holistic Spa, and she talked me into taking a few of the yoga classes. It's a mind, body, and spiritual workout," she explains.

I've taken a few yoga classes myself.

"Why do you need your own yoga room?" I ask.

"Helen, the yoga instructor at the spa, had to return to Virginia to take care of her elderly mother. So, I told the girls that I'd host yoga here once or twice a week."

"But don't you need an instructor?" I ask.

"I've got it covered, I bought videos," she states.

Videos really? That should work.

"Well, good luck with that," I tell her.

Caleb pouts. "Maybe Granna needs our help," he says.

He really doesn't want to spend the day with me.

"We can stay and help if that's what you'd rather do, bud."

"Don't be silly. It's just packing up some things on the screened-in porch and moving some furniture around. You two go have fun and bring me back a hot dog from the campground," she insists.

"Why don't you join us at the campground later?" I suggest.

"That's a great idea. I can get things done here. You two can explore and then we'll all meet back up for hot dogs. I'll call Sara-Beth and offer to make baked beans," Mom agrees.

Caleb gives in and runs upstairs to find his shoes and his tablet.

"Give him time. It'll get better," Mom tells me as she dries her hands on her apron.

"Will it? Because right now, I can't seem to say or do anything right. Maybe I should just let him do what he wants instead of forcing him to spend time with me."

"That's nonsense," she scoffs.

"No, it's not. I've done enough damage. He wanted to stay with his friends this summer. I could have let him and not uprooted us both."

"And why didn't you?" she asks.

"I was afraid he'd sit in front of a gaming console. Matthew, his friend, has older brothers, and they are always online, playing with strangers all over the world. I don't trust them. I walked in one day, and the language they used and the things they called each other were awful."

"Exactly. You can't just let a child decide for himself. Not at such a tender age. Children will clutch on to the first shiny thing that gets their attention. The wrong things and bad ideas disguised as fun are too often covered in glitter and wrapped in fanciful distraction. It's a parent's job to help them navigate the pitfalls until they are older and gain an adequate amount of maturity to recognize them for the illusions they are. Temptations are hard enough for us to resist as adults. Guiding them to wait or to trust us until then is essential. They'll have plenty of opportunities in life to learn from the consequences of poor decisions down the road. How about, for now, we just let them be children and do the heavy lifting ourselves? Even if they give us attitude. You're doing right by him," she tells me.

"I sure hope so."

"I know so," she assures me.

Caleb comes slinking down the steps, clutching his tablet and phone, with his shoes on and his earbuds in his ears.

I hold my hand out, and he looks at me.

"What?"

"Hand me the earbuds and leave the tablet and phone here," I request.

"Why?" he whines.

"Because I don't want them to distract you. We're going to have a technology-free day, enjoying nature and each other," I tell him.

He pulls the earbuds from his ears and tosses them in my hand and sets the devices on the foyer table.

"Whatever," he mumbles and storms out the door to the Volvo.

Here goes nothing.

I join him and spend the afternoon serving as his tour guide through town, and in the national forest. It's fun exploring and seeing how much things have changed and grown since the last time I was here. I regale him with stories from my childhood as I'm flooded with the memories. I introduce him around the valley, everyone treats me as if I never left and they all gush over Caleb. The concern evident in their voices as they ask the uncomfortable question again and again—how I'm doing? I just smile and politely tell them that I'm wonderful. It's a lie. I know it and so do they.

Chapter
five

Graham

"Is that Taeli?" Mom asks as the black Volvo pulls into the gate.

"Yeah. You wanted me to be nice, so I invited her and her son over, so he could meet some of the other kids," I tell her as I load the debris into the dumpster behind the office.

"That was a great idea," Mom says as she hurries over to where Taeli has parked.

She hugs her as she exits the vehicle, and they both walk around to the passenger side and wait for Caleb to emerge.

I watch as the boy grins up at her while Mom fusses over him.

She points him in the direction of the playground, and then she calls over Chris, one of the long-term campers' grandsons, and introduces them.

The boys speak for a moment, and then they take off, sprinting toward the sprinklers.

Pop makes his way over to Taeli and Mom. He hugs Taeli and kisses the top of her head. The three of them chat for a long while before she and Mom disappear into the office. I close the dumpster and head back to the pool area to finish cleaning up before the sun sets.

When they reemerge, Taeli is clutching some paperwork, and Mom is talking her ear off. Taeli's right hand comes up and shades her eyes as she looks over the grounds, searching for her son. When they catch sight of me, she smiles and waves. I wave back, and she excuses herself from Mom and makes her way over to me.

She is breathtaking. Her long, toned legs are on display in a simple cotton dress that fits her oh so well. Her sun-kissed brown hair is pulled back in a ponytail that brushes the middle of her back as she walks, and she is smiling. She and Caleb must have had a good day.

"Hey," she says as she approaches.

I stop and pull off my work gloves.

"Hey yourself. How was the afternoon, introducing Caleb around town?" I ask.

"It was good, I think. He didn't say much, but I think he liked the creek and the trolley ride. He wasn't very interested in the mountains and the views. I guess observation sites are lame or something."

"You took him to observation points?"

"Yeah. I used to love them when I was his age. Daddy would take Gene and me up to the highest points. I loved standing and looking out over the mountainside. It was thrilling, being able to see for miles and miles. I would just sit and think about how big the world was and how I wanted to see it all," she says.

"I wouldn't let it bother me that he wasn't excited. Boys like action more than quiet contemplation," I tell her.

"Hence his fondness for the creek and trolley," she agrees.

I look out to where Caleb is currently running through the sprinklers with the other kids.

"I think he's going to like his time in Balsam Ridge just fine. We tend to grow on people."

"I hope so."

"What about you? How are you, really?"

"Why does everyone keep asking me that?" she asks, clearly agitated.

I shrug. "Because they want to know how you're doing."

"No, they don't. They are just being nosy," she barks.

"Jeez, the city really jaded you," I accuse.

Offended, she points to a man standing off to the side, watching his kids play.

"Do you care how he's doing?" she asks.

"Yes. As a matter of fact, I do. He lost his wife last month but brought his kids here for vacation anyway because that's what they'd always done, and he didn't want them to lose that too. I do care if he is okay. And I stopped by his camper last night and left a basket of fresh banana bread my mom had baked to make him smile because she knew it was his favorite. I'll probably call him this weekend to see if he wants to go fishing to get him out for a while."

"Oh," she mutters, averting her eyes.

I take a step into her space, and her amber eyes come up to meet mine.

"You're going to have to retrain your brain to care about your community if you're going to live here. We aren't folks who just walk around, ignoring each other's pain," I tell her.

She sighs. "You're right. I'm jaded."

"I reckon you're allowed to be a little. Are you at least happy to be home?" I ask.

She shrugs. "It's humbling to come back. I didn't realize how much I'd missed it until I was taking Caleb around. So much has changed, yet so much is exactly as it was when I left."

"That's the way we like it," I tell her.

"Caleb kept asking me where the McDonald's and Taco Bell were," she says.

That's one of the things I love best about Balsam Ridge. We don't allow chains to come in and push out the small business owners.

"You'll have to take him to Bubba Jay's Steakhouse and ask for them to put pickles, lettuce, and Thousand Island dressing on one of their Angus burgers. It beats the fast-food stuff, hands down," I suggest.

"I'll do that. Does Bubba Jay make a dupe for the McRib too?"

I chuckle. "I'm sure he could find some pork product to mold into a rib and smother in barbeque sauce for you."

She smiles so big that a dimple pops out on her right cheek. It's the most carefree I've seen her.

Mom calls to me from the office porch. "Graham, can you light the charcoal, please?"

"Yes, ma'am," I answer. "Duty calls," I tell Taeli.

"Meet you at the picnic tables," she says and walks off toward the kids.

I help Pop man the grills while Mom, Taeli, and the other parents wrangle the children and get them dried off and washed up for dinner.

"The patch looks good, son," he says as he looks back at the empty pool.

"The tear was in a good place. I think it will hold and get you by. The glue should set overnight, but I'd give it another day. You can start filling it back up Friday morning," I suggest.

He nods.

"What do you think of Taeli?" he asks.

"Not you too, Pop," I grumble.

His brows furrow. "Huh?"

I sigh. "I think she's beautiful and smart but unsure and hard on herself. Scared and a bit lost. She feels guilty for dragging her boy across the country, and she doesn't know what to do to make it better for him," I answer.

He looks in her direction. "Wow. That's very observant, son. I was just wondering if you thought she'd be a good fit around here," he clarifies.

"Around here? What are you talking about, old man?"

"Your mom wants to hire her. We need a new employee to oversee the cabins at Rocky Pass Vacation Rentals. Your mom is spread thin between the cabins and campgrounds and managing the realty office," he says.

I turn the wieners, so they cook evenly, and lower the lid to the grill.

"You think it's worth hiring and training someone to do the job, only for them to turn around and leave at the end of the summer?" I ask him.

"That's what I told your mother, but you know how she is when she gets something in her head. She and Leona think that working might get Taeli's mind off things and help her make new friends while she's here."

"Sounds like no matter what we think, it's a done deal, but I do know from what Leona told me that she ran her husband's office. So, she's qualified," I assure him.

He nods and then slaps my back. "Yep, beautiful and smart," he repeats my observations, "exactly what our office needs."

I pile a platter with hot dogs in various states of char before throwing buns on the rack to give them a quick toasting. Mom and Taeli cover the picnic tables with paper cloths and then set out the condiments and bags of potato chips.

Leona shows up with pans of baked beans and mac 'n' cheese.

Everyone settles around the tables, and the women help the little ones add ketchup to their hot dogs.

I sit at the end of one of the tables with Pop and listen as the roar of the children's chatter and the laughter from Mom, Leona, and a few of their friends rise in the air and float back down around us.

Pop nods toward the crowd. "This is what it's all about," he says. "Yeah," I agree.

There's nothing like eating creek side with good people by the light of the stars on a cool summer evening.

Balsam Ridge might not be as exciting as Nashville or as packed as Gatlinburg, but it has a charm unmatched by any other town. That's why people always return and why some of us never leave.

Chapter
six

Taeli

"YESTERDAY WAS FUN, WASN'T IT, BUD?" I ASK CALEB AS WE head down for breakfast.

"Yeah, it was okay."

It's as good of a response as I could hope for.

"I'm thinking about taking a temporary job, helping Sara-Beth with their vacation business. That means we'll probably be spending a lot of time over at the campground."

He shrugs. "That'll be fine."

He won't ever admit that he enjoyed himself last night, playing with the other kids. *Stubborn boy.*

When we get to the landing at the bottom of the steps, Sara-Beth is at the kitchen table with Mom, enjoying a cup of coffee.

"Hi," Caleb greets as he takes a seat beside our guest.

"Good morning, Caleb."

I walk to the counter and pour myself a cup and join them.

"Sara-Beth rode up with Weston this morning," Mom explains as

I make Caleb a plate of eggs and bacon from the platters in the middle of the table.

Weston is Graham's second-youngest brother. He was behind me in school but we knew each other pretty well, as he dated many of the girls in my class, including one of my volleyball teammates.

"That's nice. I haven't seen him in forever. Where is he?" I ask.

"He's out back in the greenhouse, checking on the tomatoes," Mom answers.

It's really sweet how Sara-Beth's sons have taken Mom under their wing and stepped up to help her around here. Every morning, one or more of them show up despite their busy schedules to check in on her or to perform menial tasks for her. It's endearing.

Once I have Caleb settled and eating breakfast, I take my coffee and excuse myself to go find Weston and say hello.

A warm mountain breeze envelops me as I step out onto the porch. The aroma of honeysuckle fills the air. I can still remember plucking the flowers from the vine and pulling the small stem that runs through the bloom to get to the drop of nectar that waits inside. I'd sit for hours and lick them one after another to enjoy the sweet taste of honey.

I make my way behind the house in search of Weston and find the greenhouse door wide open. I step inside to see the long oak tables topped with potted flowers and herbs. Rows of lavender and thyme and basil lead me deeper inside, where I find him with a hand trowel, potting soil, and saplings.

His back is to me, but I can see the signature Tuttle features from here. He looks so much like Graham. His dark hair is a bit longer and curls around his collar, and he's a slightly shorter and stockier version of his older brother.

When he hears my footsteps, he turns and grins.

"Weston Tuttle, is that you?" I ask.

"Hey, Taeli. I heard you were back in town," he says as he stops his digging in the clay pots to come over and hug me.

I squeeze him back and look over his shoulder to where he was working.

"Is that what I think it is?" I ask as he releases me.

I walk over to see a row of marijuana plants growing among the tomato stalks.

"Um, no," he says.

"Weston! Are you growing weed in my mother's greenhouse?" I screech.

"Technically, I'm delivering more plants. Your mom grows them herself," he explains.

I stare at him in shock.

"Are you kidding me?" I ask.

"Nope. It's kind of her hobby, I guess you'd say."

"My mother is a pot dealer?" I ask.

"No. Absolutely not. These are strictly for personal use," he says, as if that makes it any better.

"My mother's a pothead," I mutter to myself.

"It's not like that. She doesn't smoke or anything. She just clips and boils the plants and uses them to make gummies and brownies."

That's not any better.

"Oh, she doesn't smoke it she just consumes it. That's fine then," I muse.

"Look, I own the hemp farm on the top of Trinity Gap Road. You remember where the old tater patch used to be by the river?" he asks. I nod.

That old tater patch used to supply potatoes to the entire valley when we were young.

"I bought it from Mr. Whisnet's widow a few years ago. We grow and sell one hundred percent organic CBD hemp products—oils, tinctures, gummies, et cetera. It's all legal, and it has little to no THC in it, but it has all of the medicinal benefits of cannabinoids. Our products are high quality and natural. We sell them online all over the country and in the shops in town. Everyone is trying to reap the natural benefits of hemp. It's a revolution," he explains.

I'm quite aware of the beneficial use of medical marijuana. Damon touts it's praise as an effective alternative treatment for cancer patients who experience extreme nausea due to chemotherapy. He fought diligently for it to be legalized in the state of Illinois, and it was last January; however, the bible belt states are far less progressive than the rest of the country,

"That's amazing, Weston."

"Thanks. It's been a dream of mine for a while now," he says.

So, why are you delivering plants to my mother, then?" I ask.

"Because Leona likes it a tad bit more natural than we are allowed to sell," he quips.

"Oh my God, Weston!"

I imagine my mother getting high with all her new bohemian friends and cringe.

"It's not a big deal," he insists.

I march past him, out of the greenhouse, and toward the house, where Mom and Sara-Beth are now sitting on the back deck.

"It's not that big of a deal, Taeli," Weston calls after me, but I continue forward.

"Mom, what the hell?" I screech when I make it to the front steps.

"What?" she asks.

"You can't just grow marijuana in the greenhouse!"

"Why not? It's legal now," she claims.

"Not in the state of Tennessee," I inform her.

"Really?"

"Really, Mom."

She waves me off. "Oh, well, it will be."

I climb the steps and stop in front of her chair. "Will be? That's all you have to say for yourself?"

She sighs and sets down her glass. "It's medicinal. It helps with my arthritis."

"There are medications for that," I remind her.

"Pharmaceuticals. Narcotics. Those things make me feel bad. They might help with the stiffness and pain, but they make me loopy and want to sleep all day. I don't like them."

"And getting high doesn't make you loopy?" I ask.

"I don't get high. I just have a nibble here and there. It makes me happy, and I no longer feel my knuckles," she says.

"Your knuckles?"

She makes a fist and raises it. "Enjoy the time before you start feeling your knuckles."

Sara-Beth nods in agreement.

"What?"

"There'll come a day—and it sneaks up on you—when you'll wake up and become very aware of your knuckles. For most of your life, you just walk around, not realizing they're there on your hand and how important they are. Then, suddenly, out of the blue, you feel them. Everything you do from pulling up the blanket on the bed to washing your hair or even scratching your nose requires them. They start to ache, and before you know it, they ache all the time. Then, it spreads to your knees and then your ankles. Walking hurts, sitting hurts, and even lying down hurts."

I sigh. "Mom, I don't want you to hurt."

"Then, mind your business and stay out of the greenhouse," she suggests.

My staunch Christian daddy must be rolling over in his grave. Before I can scold her any further, Caleb walks out of the back door with his phone. I can hear that he is on a video call with his father. The sound of Damon's voice causes me to shudder, but I try to control my reaction in front of Caleb.

"Mom, Dad wants to speak to you," he says.

"Tell him I'm busy right now and I'll call him back later."

He probably received the divorce papers today. My attorney sent me an email last night to warn me that they would be served at his office this morning.

Caleb tells him I'll call him later as he walks back inside.

I let out a breath.

"Avoiding Damon?" Mom asks.

"He got served today. I don't want to deal with him picking the entire filing apart," I tell them.

"It doesn't seem to me that he has a leg to stand on. He should just agree to what you want. It's the least he can do," Mom states.

"He should, " Sara-Beth agrees.

"You'd think, but I'm going after child support, alimony, the house, and half the equity in the medical practice. I know my ex, and he's boiling. I'm sure he hoped he could pay me a one-time settlement and be done with me."

"Of course he did," Sara-Beth says.

"Don't you let him bully you. I have some money in the bank, and I'll help you hire the best attorney in the state of Illinois," Mom offers.

"I can handle him, but I don't want to fight with him in front of Caleb."

It's a douche move to call our son's phone and have him bring the call to me.

"You know, signing the divorce papers doesn't make you legally obligated to hate him. Langford and his ex-wife get along splendidly," Sara-Beth tells me.

"I know that. I'll admit, in the beginning, I wanted revenge—I prayed for it—but I don't want us to hate each other. He's Caleb's father. We'll always be a part of each other's lives. All I want is what's fair and for him to step up for our son."

"That's not unreasonable," Sara-Beth agrees.

"But Damon is. He'll fight this," I mutter.

"He'll lose. Besides, you don't have to worry about revenge. Karma will catch up to him. It always does, and if you're lucky, God will give you a front-row seat when it does," Mom assures me.

My biggest fear is the only loser in this will be Caleb. He doesn't deserve to suffer for our adult choices. Yet here I am, dragging him away from where he wants to be because I can't handle the situation. I'm as much to blame for his unhappiness as Damon.

And that hurts most of all.

Chapter
seven

Graham

I DRIVE UP TO MEET WESTON AT LEONA'S HOUSE TO TAKE A LOOK AT an addition she wants to add to the back deck. I have a lot on my plate at the moment, but I find myself looking forward to going out there in hopes of seeing Taeli.

When did that happen?

The last thing I need is to get involved with her. It's a messy business to fool around with your mother's friend's daughter. Especially a daughter who is newly seperated and comes with a little person in tow. I'd be an asshole to take advantage, but there is something about her that's gotten under my skin.

I park in front and follow the voices to find them all sitting on the back deck.

"Graham," Leona calls when she sees me.

"Hi, ladies, Mom," I say as I ascend the stairs.

Taeli is standing against one of the posts with her arms folded over her chest. She is wearing a pale yellow dress with white slip-on sandals, and her hair is pulled up in a knot. And she looks tense.

"Did I interrupt anything?" I ask as I look between them.

Leona waves off the question. "Nothing important," she assures me as she stands. "I'm so happy you're here. I have everything sorted; come see."

Mom, Taeli, and I follow her as she leads us onto the upper part of the deck.

She's hung shade curtains and surrounded the room with candles and lotus flower lamps. A large stone water fountain, meant to be displayed outdoors, is plugged into the corner of the space. Vinyl Yoga Moon wall decals hang above a bamboo bench, and the floor is covered with colorful mats.

"What did you do?" Taeli asks as she looks around the screened-in room that used to be filled with comfy lounge furniture and an electric fireplace. "This was my favorite part of the house. I used to love to sit out here and read or just relax and watch the horses in the back field," she states.

"I told you I was making a yoga room. I think it's fun and whimsical," Leona announces.

"It's tacky, Mom," Taeli disagrees.

"When did you become such a fuddy-duddy?" Leona asks her daughter.

Taeli looks offended. "I'm not. I'm sensible. This is a great outdoor space, and you ruined it."

"*Sensible* is just another word for prude. I didn't raise you to be a snob, young lady," Leona retorts.

Mom and I exchange a look, and I try to hold back my laughter as they continue to bicker.

"Yeah, well, I didn't expect you to turn into such a hippie. What happened to my mother?"

"You say that like it's an insult. I embrace my inner hippie. Life is too short to be walking around with a chip on your shoulder and acting like a stick in the mud," Leona scolds before turning her attention to me.

"Now, Graham, what I'd like to do is replace the screens with glass panels that roll up like garage doors so that we can have the space open when the weather allows but still use the space when the winter temperatures hit. Also, I'm thinking of hanging mirrors across this wall and painting it all a calming blue," Leona explains.

Taeli looks on with a befuddled expression before shaking her head and walking into the house.

Once Leona has finished explaining her vision to me, I promise to have some plans drawn up with a quote estimate for her by the end of next week. Then, I head out in search of Taeli.

I find her in the front yard, barefoot, twirling in the tire swing.

"Having fun?" I ask.

"I don't know my own mother," she says.

I lean against the trunk of the tree and watch her spin.

"I don't know my son either," she continues.

I stand there in silence and let her talk it out.

"I obviously didn't know my husband. How did I let this happen?"

It's a rhetorical question.

"I gave him everything. The best parts of me. I lost my self-worth because of him. What's left?"

I laugh.

She digs her feet into the ground to bring herself to a halt, and her angry eyes bore into me.

"You think that's funny?" she asks.

"It's called self-worth, Taeli. That means the value and love you have for yourself. The pride you have in who you are. No one can take that from you or alter it. It's who you see when you look in the mirror.

Stop looking at yourself through everyone else's eyes. You know who you are, and their opinions can't change that," I tell her.

"You don't even know me," she retorts.

"Maybe I don't, but I do know Leona. She's kind, funny, and a bit quirky, but she has a big heart. She's been dealt some hard blows in life, same as you. You should get to know her."

"Same as me, huh? My husband didn't die. He ripped our family apart on purpose."

"It still feels the same. She's grieving. You're grieving. The only difference is, she is choosing to move forward, and you are choosing to continue feeling sorry for yourself," I accuse.

"You want to take me to dinner?" she asks.

"I do."

"I'll be ready in five," she says. She hops out of the swing and hurries into the house, passing Mom and Weston as she goes.

Mom's eyes follow her inside and then come back to me.

"We're going to dinner," I blurt out.

Mom grins, and Weston's eyebrows rise.

"How did that happen?" he asks.

"I have no idea."

Chapter
eight

Taeli

D**ID I JUST ASK GRAHAM TUTTLE TO TAKE ME ON A DATE? WHAT WAS** *I thinking?*

I wasn't. There's no other explanation. One minute, he was lecturing me, and the next, I was demanding he feed me.

I stand in front of the bathroom mirror and take in my appearance. Dark circles and unruly hair.

Perfect.

"It's not like he hasn't already seen you, Taeli," I scold my reflection.

Okay, quick damage control is in order.

I turn the faucet on to the hottest setting, grab a hand towel from the linen closet, and steam my face. Then, I dab concealer under my eyes and add tinted moisturizer, bronzer, a couple of coats of mascara, and raspberry lip gloss. I pull my hair from the knot, run my fingers through it, and spritz on some perfume.

I take the damp towel and run it over my feet before I slip them back into my sandals.

On my way back down the stairs, I run into Mom.

"Where are you off to in such a hurry?" she asks.

"I'm going to dinner with Graham."

Her eyes go wide. "Isn't it early for dinner?" she asks.

"Yeah, maybe," I say nervously.

"I'm sure you'll find something to do until it's time to eat. Don't worry about Caleb. I'll take him on a Granna date to the arcade tonight."

"Thanks," I say before continuing to the door.

"Taeli?" she calls, and I turn to look up at her. "You look beautiful. Have fun."

She winks at me.

Graham is waiting by his truck when I make it out to the porch.

I hesitate as I watch him clean some paperwork off of the passenger seat and toss it in the back of the cab.

My heart is racing. I take a couple of deep breaths to calm myself.

It's just two friends spending the evening together, I tell myself.

When Graham notices me, he smiles and opens the door wider, beckoning me.

Here goes nothing.

I trot down the steps and take his offered hand. He helps me up into the raised truck, then rounds the front and joins me.

"Where to?" he asks as he starts the engine.

"Anywhere. Let's just drive," I request.

A grin spreads across his lips. "We can do that."

He pulls out of the drive and heads toward town, but when we reach the valley, he takes a right turn, and we start climbing again.

"Where are we going?" I ask.

"On an adventure."

He drives us up the back side of the mountain, deep into the woods. The gravel road is narrow, and the ascension is steep. There isn't much out here, but the view is spectacular.

"I forgot how beautiful it is here in the summer," I say as I reach for the button to roll down my window. Cool, fresh air floods the cab, and I rest my chin on my arm that's propped on the windowsill.

The warm afternoon sun kisses my skin, and I close my eyes. It's like I'm sixteen again. The sound of gravel crunching under the tires, the babble of the water rolling over rocks in the creek below, the soft song of the breeze rustling through the trees.

I open one eye and look over to Graham, who is watching me instead of the road ahead.

"I didn't realize that I'd missed this," I confess.

We come to a private entrance at the top of the mountain, and he brings the truck to a stop. I sit up and watch as he hits a button clipped to his sun visor, and the massive iron gate begins to open.

"Where are we?" I ask.

"My place," he says.

We wind our way up to a modern, large Swiss chalet home perched above the tree line. The house is gorgeous. The front of the two-story structure is almost completely glass. Framed in rich, dark wood. A covered deck wraps around the main level, and the carved support beams lead down to a patio with a stone fireplace. The roof is gabled with wide eaves and exposed construction beams—perfect for surviving heavy snowfall.

"You live in a ski resort," I muse.

He chuckles.

"Not quite, but I did model the design off of an Alpine lodge," he says as he pulls up in front of a detached three-bay garage.

I sit there in awe, staring up at the beautiful home.

He hits another button, and one of the dark wood garage doors slides open to reveal a matte-black Harley-Davidson.

"Come on," he says as he exits the truck.

I open my door, hop down, and follow him into the garage.

When I make it by his side, he picks me up off of my feet and sets me down on the bike.

"I'm wearing a dress," I say as I straddle the seat.

He shrugs.

"I've never been on a motorcycle before," I admit.

"I'm glad I get to be your first," he says smugly.

"Graham, are you sure you know how to drive this thing?" I ask the stupid question. He owns it, so he obviously knows how to operate it.

He walks over and grabs a helmet off of a hook. He places it on my head and tightens the chin strap. I reach up and clasp his wrist. His eyes come to mine, and he grins.

"Don't be nervous. You're in good hands."

He secures his helmet and puts on a pair of wraparound sunglasses. Then, he takes a seat in front of me. I fist the front of the dress and scoot closer to him.

"Rest your knees against my hips and wrap your arms around me," he instructs.

I do just that, and he tugs me forward, flush against his back.

"Now, relax and trust me. Lean with me and the bike. I'll handle the rest," he says before cranking the beast.

The low rumble of the engine and the vibration of power between my legs cause a thrill to shoot through me. I squeeze him and bury my face in his neck as he hits the gas, and we take off.

Graham keeps us at a slow and steady pace as we descend the mountain, very careful not to jolt me around too much, but once we reach the paved road of the valley, he lets loose, and we fly.

It's exhilarating.

We make our way out of town and onto one of the scenic Smoky Mountain byways and cruise. He makes a point to stop at every observation lookout, so I can take in the views. At one point, we are so high that the clouds settle around us like a mist.

By the time the sun starts to set, I'm as comfortable on the back of his bike as I am seated in the passenger side of a truck. I loosen my grip on him and raise my arms into the air, letting the wind whip through the ends of my hair peeking beneath the helmet, flying around me.

We navigate off the byway to this quaint little restaurant tucked into the side of the mountain and stop. Graham helps me off the bike, we remove our helmets and we make our way inside. We are greeted by a hostess, and Graham requests a table next to a window.

As she leads us into the restaurant, Graham tells me that we are one mile up.

We stop at a table that is draped in white linens. It's beautiful but pales in comparison to the breathtaking panoramic views overlooking the mountain range outside the floor-to-ceiling windows.

"Graham," I gasp.

"I thought you'd like it," he says as he pulls a chair out for me.

"It's stunning."

And romantic.

He leans down and whispers in my ear, "Wait until you taste the lobster bisque."

He orders a bottle of wine, and I let him make our dinner selections. He orders a few dishes he wants me to try, and he is obviously excited to introduce me to his favorites.

"I'm sorry I forced you into spending the day with me," I tell him, a little embarrassed.

"You didn't force me to do anything."

"I put you on the spot," I point out.

He pauses for a moment.

"Yeah, you kind of did," he teases, as the server returns with our glasses.

"I'm having a really nice time," I tell him.

He reaches over the table and takes my hand. He holds it and lightly runs his thumb in a circle on the inside of my wrist. I'm terrified he can feel the increase of my pulse.

"So am I. It's nice to step away from work and enjoy the countryside. Living here, I think we sometimes forget to appreciate the beauty. We take it for granted. Today was a reminder of why I love home so much," he confesses.

I take a sip of my wine and swallow down the lump of emotion in my throat. He just verbalized what I'd been contemplating all day.

How did I ever feel suffocated here?

I look out the windows at the beautiful view.

"I envy trees," I say.

His brow creases.

"Why?"

"Because when it's time to change, they do. They let their leaves glow bright with color in autumn, and then, come winter, they let them go so easily to make room for new growth in the spring. New adventure. New purpose." I muse.

His eyes follow mine out to the landscape.

"Yeah, I guess they do."

Our entrees arrive a moment later and we enjoy our candlelit meal.

"Try this."

He raises a spoon to my lips.

I close my eyes as the smooth, velvety texture of the rich soup hits my tongue.

"Oh my God, that's amazing," I tell him.

"Right? It's the best I've ever had."

Graham did an excellent job with all his selections. Every mouthful is better than the last.

I learn all there is to know about his family while we eat. Each of his brothers has chosen very different career paths. Langford is spearheading the new ski resort in Balsam Ridge, Corbin is the chief of Valley Fire and Rescue, Weston has his organic CBD farm, Garrett is the country music star, and Morris—the baby—is still at home with his parents, trying to figure out what he wants from life.

I sigh. "Your family is not real."

"Why do you say that?" he asks.

"Y'all are too perfect. Real families are messy."

"That's awfully cynical and presumptuous. We are far from perfect. Langford is divorced. Garrett can't hold down a real relationship; he just moves from groupie to groupie. I'm a widower, and Morris is twenty-seven and still lives with his mother."

I giggle. "Okay, so not perfect, but close enough."

We finish our meal, Graham pays the bill, and we head back out to the motorcycle. The evening air is crisp and chilly.

"I didn't think this through," he says as his eyes gaze my sleeveless arms.

He unbuttons his flannel shirt and removes it, revealing a tightly fitted tee underneath. "Here, put this on," he instructs.

I take the shirt and pull it on. It swallows me, but it's warm, and it smells of him. I bury my nose into the collar and inhale.

"Aren't you going to be cold?" I ask.

"Not if you snuggle in close," he says.

I can do that.

We make our way back to Mom's house, guided by the moonlight. Graham takes it much slower this time, trying to block the cold air from me with his massive frame. I snuggle into his back, tuck my face into his neck, and hold him close, hoping my warmth is seeping into his bones.

When we pull into the drive, he dismounts, and I follow. He helps me remove the helmet, and he runs his fingers through my tangled hair.

I'm anxious as we stand there.

Should I invite him in? Leave him standing here and run inside? Thank him yet again?

He doesn't give me a chance to do any of those things. He brings his lips to mine and kisses me. I gasp with surprise, and he takes the opportunity to deepen the kiss. His mouth is soft and inviting, and I step closer into him as I clutch the front of his shirt and kiss him back. I'm not sure how long we are locked together, but I finally break away and blink up at him.

"You kissed me."

"I did."

"Why did you kiss me?"

He shrugs. "Kissing reduces anxiety, and you looked a little stressed to me."

"So, you kissed me to calm me down?"

"Yep."

"You can't just go around, kissing anyone," I scold.

He leans in. "I don't. I kiss who I want to kiss," he says before laying one more quick kiss on my lips.

All righty then.

I walk past him and toward the porch in a daze.

"See you tomorrow, Taeli," he calls.

I throw my hand up in acknowledgment but don't turn back around as I hear the motorcycle roar to life and pull away.

Mom is at the door when I walk inside.

"Did you have a good time?"

"Magical," I admit.

She smiles wide.

"It looks like it. Is that Graham's shirt?" she asks.

I look down. I'm still wrapped in his flannel.

"Oh, I should have given this back to him."

"No worries. I think you'll get the chance," Mom says.

I hope so.

Chapter
nine

Taeli

MOM GRILLED ME ABOUT MY DAY SPENT WITH GRAHAM. I GAVE her the details, leaving out the kissing part, and hurried off to bed, where I stripped off my dress and pulled his shirt back on. I lay awake most of the night, surrounded by his smell and freaking out about said kiss.

In the morning, I get Caleb up and dressed early, and we head to meet Sara-Beth at the Rocky Pass offices before they open. I fill out some paperwork, and she shows me the ropes.

It all seems fairly basic with most reservations coming through the website.

"We have cabins of various sizes sprinkled throughout the mountains with different views. Our largest rental is an eight-bed, six-bath cabin, and our smallest is a studio-style riverside fishing cabin. All are pet-friendly, and we have a minimum of two-night stays. As long as there is no damage, the security deposit is refunded after maintenance inspects the cabin after checkout."

She hands me a sheet of paper with a list of other vacation rental companies and campsites in the valley: Balsam Ridge Vacations, Mountain Escape Rentals, Stoneridge RV Resort, Cool Breeze Campground and Creekside Motor Village.

"If we fill up or don't have a cabin that suits someone's occupancy needs, please refer them to one of those contacts to help them find a place."

I love that they support other local businesses.

"We usually do direct deposit for employees, but since you're temporary, for now, I'll cut you a check every Friday."

She shows me how to log in to the computer and gives me a map, showing all the rental properties and their names. Then, she, Caleb, and I climb into her vehicle to drive around to some of the locations.

She opens one of the larger cabins, and we take a look around.

"We provide the linens, and the kitchens are fully stocked with all the cookware, dishes, mugs, and wineglasses they could need. All cabins come furnished with gas grills and outdoor firepits. Some have hot tubs on the decks, and some don't. For the ones with them, we supply bathrobes and spa towels. If a guest calls the office, requesting anything additional, just forward the inquiry to maintenance, and they'll handle it," she tells me as we walk around the space.

"In the winter, we do get calls for firewood. It's not something we generally provide, but the roads can get a bit tricky, and I'd rather one of the boys bring a load up than for guests to try to navigate their way down on icy roads at night."

I'll be back in Chicago by the time the snowy season begins, but I don't point that out.

We stop for lunch on the way back, and Mom joins us. She takes Caleb with her to do some gem mining. He is less than thrilled, but he doesn't complain. Once we are back in the car, Sara-Beth continues with her instruction.

"The cabins have combination locks that we change after every stay, so most guests will go straight to their location. We do get an occasional walk-in of someone who's just passing through and decides to stay. If they only want one night, direct them to any of the motels in town. If they want to book a cabin and the receptionist is in the office, you can have them follow you to show them a property. Speak of the devil," she says as we pull back into the office parking lot.

As we exit Sara-Beth's car and head toward the office, a woman with shoulder-length brown hair descends the office's steps and meets us in the lot.

"Hi, Sara-Beth, I was just heading out for lunch. Can I get you anything?"

"No, we just ate. Erin, this is Taeli. She's going to be taking over the cabin rentals. Taeli, Erin is the receptionist for the realty company. She helps me keep the agents in line," Sara-Beth introduces us.

"TT? Is that you?"

I give her a tight smile of acknowledgment.

Erin and I went to high school together. We were pretty close back in the day, but we haven't spoken much the past few years.

"Nobody calls me that anymore. It's just Taeli now," I correct her.

"I didn't realize you two knew each other. That's wonderful," Sara-Beth says.

"We go way back," Erin tells her.

A phone rings from inside, and Sara-Beth hurries up the steps.

"I'll get that. You two catch up," she says.

Once she's inside, Erin turns back to me.

"Well, look at you. I didn't think you'd ever come back to this one-horse town. How are you? How's the big city and that handsome husband of yours? Tell me everything!"

"I'm fine. The city is fine. My husband is a lying, cheating jackass. And that about sums up my life at the moment. What about you?" I word-vomit all over her.

She just stares at me with her mouth agape and blinks for a beat.

"Girl, it sounds like you and I took the same cruise on a sinking ship. I married a handsome devil with a wandering eye after graduation myself. He was a smooth, double-talking snake from Alabama, and I was clueless until the rumor mill started churning. My inbox began lighting up like the Fourth of July. He tried to deny it all, but in a small town like Balsam Ridge, nobody is going to let a no-good cheater get away with making a fool of one of its own."

Now, it is my turn to stare.

I forgot how open everyone in Balsam Ridge is. In my suburban life of luncheons and dinner parties, people only portrayed themselves and their lives in the best light. Even if your marriage was on the brink of falling into ruin, you did everything to pretend it wasn't to save face. I never realized how exhausting it was to keep up the facade until now. Having Erin just blurt out the messy truth of her life is surprisingly refreshing.

"My husband was boinking his assistant, which isn't unheard of, but he was stupid enough to knock her up," I share.

She shakes her head. "What a dumb bastard," she says without a hint of judgment in her voice.

"I think my son hates me," I continue.

She holds her hand up to stop me.

"Oh, please. How old is he, thirteen, fourteen?" she asks.

"Twelve," I answer.

"Close enough. All teenagers hate their parents. It's practically a biological response at that age," she assures me.

I think back to my tumultuous relationship with my own mother.

Oh God, please tell me it won't last that long.

"Do you know what you need?" Erin asks, bringing me out of my thoughts.

"What?"

"A girls' night out. I'll rally some of the girls together, and we'll go blow off some steam. You remember Jena and Ansley from high school, don't you?" she asks as she fishes her phone from her back pocket and starts typing.

"I don't know, Erin. I'm not sure I'll be great company."

She waves me off. "You don't have to be good company. We'll be the good company you need at the moment."

"But …"

"But nothing. I've already sent up the bat signal. Go and arrange a sitter and be ready by six. We'll pick you up. Are you at your mom's place?"

"Yeah."

"Cool. See you after lunch," she says before she walks off toward her car.

I guess I'm going out tonight.

When Erin returns, Sara-Beth leaves the two of us to head to a closing.

Erin gives me a more in-depth overview of the office and computer system.

Graham and Hilton stop by, and my heart rate picks up when I spy Graham coming up from the parking lot.

Get yourself together, Taeli.

Erin notices my loss of focus and follows my attention to the door.

She nudges me with her elbow when Graham walks through the threshold.

"Ouch," I say, snapping my gaze to her.

"Caught you looking," she teases.

I shush her as the men stop in front of the desk.

"Hey, gals," Hilton greets.

"Hi, Mr. T, Graham," Erin replies.

"Hi," Graham says to me.

"Hi."

Hilton watches his son and me stare each other down for a few beats, and then he clears his throat.

"Graham and I were on our way to a construction site and thought we'd drop by to see how your first day was going and ask if you needed anything."

I look up at him and smile.

"Things are going great," Erin interjects. "She's a natural. I think she already has a better handle on the system than I do."

"That's wonderful," Hilton declares.

"Um, Mr. T, one of the campers called in a maintenance order this morning because their water pressure was extremely low. Can you come and take a look at it?" Erin asks.

Hilton follows her over to her desk.

"Sounds like you fit right in around here," Graham observes.

"Offices are my thing," I blurt out the absurdity.

He chuckles.

"Where's Caleb?" he asks.

"With Mom. She's dragging him to a gem mine. He's probably going to want to kill me when he gets home."

"Mining can be fun," he says.

"Please, mining is a silly tourist trap. He's going to hate it."

"Probably, yeah," he agrees.

"And on top of that, Erin has roped me into some *girls' night out, high school reunion* thing tonight. Which means leaving him with my mother for the second night in a row."

"I'll let you in on a little secret: children usually enjoy time with their grandmothers," he whispers.

"Not mine. They barely know each other, and you've met my mother."

"I have. She's a lot of fun, and I'm sure she is doing her best to spoil Caleb rotten."

I frown.

"Go have fun with the girls. I'll check in on Caleb later," he offers.

"You will?" I ask.

"Yeah, I have to take some measurements of the screened-in porch anyway."

"Thank you, Graham," I say as Erin and Hilton rejoin us.

Graham winks at me.

"You ready to head out, son?" Hilton asks.

"Right behind you, Pop."

They leave, and no sooner do their boots hit the gravel than Erin pulls a chair up beside me.

"What was that all about?" she asks.

"Nothing," I say as I stand and walk off to the file room.

"It sure didn't look like nothing to me," she calls after me.

Chapter
ten

Taeli

I WAS WRONG. CALEB DIDN'T HATE THE GEM MINE. HE LOVED IT. When I got home from work, he was sitting at my mother's table with an assortment of rocks he had collected and a copy of *The Gemstone Bible*, searching through the pages to identify his finds.

"Look at this one. It's called a tourmaline, and it's supposed to soothe panic attacks. And this one is smoky quartz, and it is grounding and helps stabilize negative emotions," he says proudly as he shows off his rocks.

"Wow, that's beautiful," I tell him.

He picks up another with a honey-colored hue.

"This one is my favorite. It's topaz, and it symbolizes honesty, forgiveness, and truth. It matches your eyes," he says as he places the rough stone in my hand.

I fight back tears as I wrap my fingers around it.

"It's lovely," I tell him before dropping it back in his palm to add to his pile of treasures.

"Granna said she knows a jeweler in town who can polish them and make them shine. She's going to take me tonight to eat pizza, and we're going to show him all of these."

"She is?"

That was too easy.

He nods.

"I'm sorry you can't come," he says.

"I can't? Why not?" I ask, feigning hurt.

"It's a secret," he says.

Mom comes in and looks over my shoulder.

"He's quite the miner," she muses.

"Are you sure you don't want me to take him for pizza tonight?" I ask.

Caleb's panicked eyes snap up to hers.

"No, we are on a Granna-grandson mission. No mothers allowed," she confirms and winks at him. Then, she whispers to me, "Sara-Beth called. You enjoy your night with the girls."

"Thanks, Mom," I say over my shoulder as we both watch him find another one of his gems in the book.

I decide it's time to put a little effort into my appearance. So, I fish out a pair of skinny jeans, a fitted white Alizeh crop top with a tie closure on the side, and a pair of camel-colored ankle booties from the closet. I go a little heavier on the makeup, adding a light foundation, eyelash extensions, and a bold red lip. I curl the ends of my hair and add a tan leather headband to hold it away from my face.

I stand back and inspect the finished product in the full-length mirror hanging on the back of my bedroom door.

Not bad.

I feel more like myself than I have in a long time as I throw my ID, credit card, and lipstick into my cream clutch and head downstairs.

I pour myself a glass of Malbec and wait for the girls. Erin texted that she was picking up Jena and Ansley, another girl we went to high school with, and they were on their way about twenty minutes ago.

I was apprehensive about this get-together. It's not exactly the triumphant homecoming I envisioned, but now that I've got my mission outfit and face on, I'm actually looking forward to the evening.

I finish my wine and place the glass in the sink when I hear the horn blaring outside.

We take a seat at our table, and Erin orders a bucket of craft beer and a plate of nachos.

"Can I have your wine list?" I ask the waitress.

"We have a house white and a house red," she answers.

"Just the two?" I ask.

"Just the two," she confirms.

"I'll take a glass of the red," I order.

"Me too," Jena adds.

The waitress turns to Ansley.

"I'm splitting the bucket with Erin, but I'll take a frosted mason jar and some orange slices, please."

"You got it. I'll be back with your drinks and the nachos in a minute, and then I'll get your order."

She walks off toward the bar, and we look over the menu.

"What's good?" I ask.

"The place is called Barbecue and Brews. I'd suggest the barbecue and the beer," Erin deadpans.

Jena and Ansley giggle.

"I'm not a beer drinker," I confess.

"I'm not either, but ever since the Appalachian Ridge Brewery opened, I've been trying the craft beers they bottle, and some are really good," Jena informs me.

"Then, why did you order wine?" I ask.

"I didn't want you to feel like the odd duck, drinking wine alone. But I'm warning you: the house wine here is a step down from domestic beer."

Great.

"We'll let you try ours, and then you'll know if you can acquire a taste or not," Ansley suggests.

Our drinks hit the table, and we place our dinner orders. They were right; the wine is shit, so I decide to try the beer. It isn't awful. After the third bottle, it actually starts tasting pretty good.

"Fill me in. I want to hear all about your lives," I tell them, partly to get the attention off of me, but mostly because I want to know.

Jena speaks up first. "I married Phillip after graduation. You remember him, don't you?"

I nod. They dated on and off all through our middle and high school years.

"That lasted for about a year before he began drinking to excess, and we started fighting all the time. I finally got fed up and divorced him. That's when I met Trent," she explains.

"And Trent is?" I ask.

"My current husband. We've been together for fifteen years now, and we have an eight-year-old daughter. Trent owns Mountainscapes Landscaping, Tree Removal, and View Enhancements, and I work for Tuttle and Sons Realty in the Luxury Mountain Homes Division."

"She's good at it too. She outsells the other agents three to one," Erin adds.

I turn to her. "What about you?" I ask.

She told me she was on her second marriage too.

"My first husband was cheating on me with one of his friends' wives. It went on for a while unnoticed until one of her co-workers spied them together after hours, and word got out. When the talk finally reached my ears, I confronted him. He denied it for a while, but he eventually fessed up. I kicked his ass out, and I moved into one of the apartments out beside the fairgrounds. Ted moved into the apartment three doors down later that year. He's a big ole bear of a man who works for the Department of Fish and Wildlife, and there was just something about him that made my pulse race. Before I knew it, I was at the altar again."

"So, you're all happily married now?" I ask.

"Except for Ansley. She's too busy pining over Garrett Tuttle to give any other man a chance," Jena says.

"I am not pining over Garrett!" Ansley protests.

"Right. You haven't so much as batted an eyelash at another man since he took off to Nashville," Erin says.

"That's not true. I've dated a few people. I just haven't married any of them. I figure I'll just skip that first bad marriage all of you had and go straight into that second good one."

"That's not a bad plan. I wish I'd thought of it. It would have saved me a lot of trouble," I say.

"Yeah, she found out her husband was fooling around and knocked up his assistant," Erin tells them.

"Y'all want to know the most pathetic part?" I ask.

Erin leans in and starts rolling her hand in invitation. "Lay it on us."

"It wasn't the first time. About a year before, I caught him in a hotel room with an X-ray tech."

They gasp.

"You did?" Ansley asks.

I nod.

"Yep. He was in Chicago for a conference. I usually accompany him for those, but Caleb had a band recital that weekend, so I stayed home, and he went alone. During the recital, I got an emergency call from Damon's mother. His father was having chest pains, and she had called an ambulance. She was frantic and wanted Damon and me to meet them at the hospital. So, I left Caleb with one of the other band moms, and I started calling Damon. His phone just rang and went straight to voice mail. I figured he was probably mingling with colleagues at the hotel after their meeting, so I drove straight into the city and decided to pick him up on the way to Northwestern Memorial Hospital.

"When I got to the Palmer House, I valeted and ran to the desk to find out what room he was in. I had my ID out and told the clerk who I was, and before I could say another word, she started apologizing. She said, 'Oh, Mrs. Lowder, we're so sorry you had to come down. We were just about to deliver the extra towels you requested.' Confused, I said there was no need and I could take them myself. She waved over a worker who had an armful of towels, and I took them. Then, I looked back to her and said I walked out of my room without my key, so she told the other desk clerk to make me a new key for suite 2026. I took the room key and the towels, and I rushed up the elevator.

"When I entered his room, a woman was in the bed, and she sat up and let out a scream before yelling at me that I shouldn't just enter their room without knocking. Damon ran from the bathroom, fresh from his shower, and I threw the towels at him as he started trying to explain that it wasn't what I thought."

"Did you kick him in the balls?" Jena asks.

I halt my tale and blink in her direction.

"Did you?" she asks again.

"No," I answer.

"Why the hell not? He was standing there in his birthday suit; it was the perfect opportunity to nail his nuts," Erin interjects.

"I didn't think to. I just wanted him to get dressed and for us to get out of there."

"You should have kicked his ass, broken his legs, or something, and then loaded him up to go to the hospital. You were already headed that way," Jena adds.

"I didn't have time to process. I was in concerned daughter-in-law mode."

Erin shrugs. "Sucks you missed the chance."

"Yeah, hindsight," I agree.

"Then, what happened?" Ansley pushes me to continue.

I take a deep breath.

"I told him about his dad and demanded he got dressed," I say.

"What did the tramp do?" Erin asks.

"She leaped from the bed and wrapped her arms around him to console him."

"The nerve!" Ansley screeches.

"I hope you yanked her hair out of her head," Jena squeals.

"Did you kick her in the twat?" Erin asks.

I shake my head.

"Dammit," Erin bellows.

"I know. I should have done all of that. Instead, I picked him up and drove him to the hospital, where we spent the night comforting his mother and praying for his father, who ended up having bypass surgery. Damon was in doctor mode, and I was caught up in the emotional support role. By the time his father was home and recovering at our house, it all got shoved under the rug. Damon apologized. Said it had never happened before and would never happen again, and I was stupid enough to believe him."

The table goes silent for a moment.

"The worst part is, I'd worked so hard to keep us afloat all those years. We only had one child because we couldn't handle more at the time. Hell, Caleb was raised by television and video games while we both worked our asses off. We were finally in a place where we were going to start reaping the rewards. The practice was thriving, and we both had more time. Time to be a family, to travel, to make Caleb the priority. I didn't want to throw that away over one indiscretion, so I forced myself to believe him. How pathetic does that make me?"

Erin sighs. "Yeah, well, we've all been stupid before. I believed my first husband too, at first."

"So did I. I believed him when he said he was going to stop drinking," Jena adds.

"You did?" I ask.

"Yep. You can't beat yourself up for wanting to save your marriage, Taeli. And no one should judge you for trying to work things out and getting burned again," Jena says.

"Least of all us," Erin agrees.

Our orders arrive, and I enjoy the best beef brisket and baked beans that I've ever had. This place might look like a dive, but the service and food quality are impressive.

Several patrons make their way to our table to say hello, and the girls introduce me to everyone like we are the best of friends.

It's nice to spend the evening just being me. Not Damon's wife.

We dance, play a round of darts, order another bucket of beers, and settle back in at our table.

"I want to know one thing," Jena says, leaning over the table and taking my hand.

"What's that?" I ask.

"Why in the hell are you still wearing your wedding rings?"

She holds up my hand to show the diamond and band on my finger.

I look at the set through my beer-soaked eyes and frown.

Why am I still wearing them?

"I don't know. Habit?" I answer.

"Habit? Girl, it's been months. How are any of these fine men going to know you are available for rebound sex if you have that dick-head's rings on?" Erin asks as she gestures around the bar.

"Are you even sure you want a divorce?" Jena asks.

"Yes, I'm sure," I say.

"Really sure?" Erin asks.

"One hundred percent sure," I insist.

She looks at Jena and grins. "I think she's ready."

Jena nods her agreement, and then they both look at me.

"Ready for what?" I ask.

"A ring toss," Erin says.

"Oh boy," Ansley says.

"Finish your beers, ladies. I'll grab the check," Jena instructs before waving down our waitress.

Chapter eleven

Taeli

"I DIDN'T WEAR THE RIGHT SHOES FOR THIS," ANSLEY says as the four of us hold on to one another, trying not to fall down the hill behind the bar that leads into the woods.

It's dark ahead, except for the light from Erin's phone and what looks to be a porch light glowing in between the trees in the distance.

I stumble over a rock or log or something large, and Jena tugs my arm to pull me off my ass. The ground is damp, and my ankle boots are sinking into the soft earth.

"We're almost there," Erin calls.

"Almost where?" I ask.

"You'll see," Jena says as she urges me forward.

A few minutes later, we are standing on the bank of Balsam Creek. Which is a large stream that runs off of the Coyote River and flows through the middle of the valley.

I look at the rushing water and back to them.

Erin holds her hand out to me.

"What?"

"Hand over the rings," she demands.

I look down at my left hand. At the beautiful five-carat diamond ring that Damon gifted me on our fifteenth wedding anniversary to replace the small one he'd proposed with when we were poor college kids. The one he bought for me after I caught him in the hotel room with another woman. The apology ring he slid on my finger, recommitting himself to me and our marriage.

The guilt ring.

I yank them off and move to hand them to her, and she catches my hand.

"Are you sure you're done with that no-good, lying, cheating, vow-breaking son of a bitch?" she asks.

"Yep," I tell her without hesitation.

She grins and wraps my fingers around the rings. "Then, toss them," she says.

I glance down at her fingers clasped around mine and back up.

"Trust me, it's liberating," she says.

Jena and Ansley cheer me on, and I step past Erin to the water's edge.

I let loose the tears that I've been holding back, and as they begin to glide hot down my cheeks, I rear back and throw them as hard as I can into the flow.

Erin, Jena, and Ansley all start cheering and whistling as the rings hit the surface.

Before I know it, I'm enveloped by them, and we are jumping and laughing.

"How did that feel?" Jena asks.

"It felt good," I shout.

"Right? I brought Erin out here to do the same thing when she found out Scott was cheating on her," she tells me.

Ansley giggles, getting our attention. "I just imagine some

fisherman gutting the trout he caught and finding a diamond ring inside. Like finding a pearl in an oyster."

"Yeah, a twenty-thousand-dollar pearl," I say through my laughter.

Erin's head snaps to me. "What did you say?"

"Huh?"

She points to the dark water. "Did you say that those rings were worth twenty grand?"

"Yes. Well, the diamond ring is," I confirm.

Her eyes go wide.

"The fuck you say?!" she shouts before she scrambles into the water and starts flailing around.

"What are you doing?" I ask.

"Getting that ring. Are you insane? Help me," she demands, and we all jump in after her.

The four of us futilely swim around, searching the murky water for the rings. It's a useless endeavor.

"Dammit," Erin says as we pull ourselves to the bank.

We are all soaked, freezing, and exhausted.

"The current probably has that thing all the way to Nashville by now," Ansley gasps.

"Or it's in some fish's belly," Jena agrees.

Erin smacks me on the arm.

"Ouch. What was that for?" I ask.

"What moron throws a twenty-thousand-dollar ring in the creek?" she screeches.

"You told me to. You said it would be liberating!" I remind her.

"That's because I thought it was just a regular wedding set, not one that could buy you a new car. You should have told me to kiss your ass, tucked the rock into your pocket, and tossed the wedding band only. It could have been symbolic."

"You didn't offer a symbolic toss," I grumble.

One minute, we are yelling at one another, and the next minute, we are screaming in fear as a bright spotlight is flashed in our eyes.

We look up through squinted eyes to see a man with a flashlight held steady on us.

He doesn't say anything as he takes in the muddy, drenched four-some huddled on the water's edge in the middle of the night.

"Officer?" Jena asks in a whisper.

He lowers the light, and our eyes adjust to see Graham Tuttle standing before us, fighting to keep from bursting into laughter.

"Shit," I mutter.

"What are you doing here?" Erin asks.

"Dad got a call from one of the cabins, complaining about a bunch of loud, drunk teenagers out in the woods. He asked me to come check it out for him," he explains.

"Loud? We weren't loud," Jena protests.

He chuckles. "I could hear you yelling and splashing around from the road," he informs us.

"We aren't drunk," Erin declares.

He gives her a look.

She points to Ansley and changes her statement. "Well, Ansley isn't drunk."

Ansley lifts her hand and holds her fingers about an inch apart. "Maybe this much drunk," she admits.

"Are we in trouble?" I ask.

He grins. "If you guys are done with your midnight swim, I think we can let it slide this time," he teases.

I let out a breath. "Oh, thank goodness. I can't call my mom to get me out of jail again," I say.

All their eyes come to me.

"You guys remember Senior Day?"

Then, they all start nodding, and we collapse in a fit of giggles.

Graham just watches us.

"All right, ladies, let's get you all home," he says as he pulls his phone from his back pocket.

He dials. "Hey, Ted. I just fished your wife and her friends out of the creek down behind the barbecue joint. Okay, we'll be waiting up by my truck. I'll get them dried off."

He ends the call and holds out his hand. I take it, and he helps me to my feet.

I stumble into his chest.

His warm, hard chest.

I look up into his amused eyes.

"Don't tell my mom about this," I whisper.

He leans in and says, "It's our little secret," and a shiver prickles down my spine as his hot breath tickles my ear.

A throat clears, and I quickly turn to see Erin, Jena, and Ansley grinning at us.

"Follow me, ladies, and watch your step," he instructs as he takes my hand.

I reach back and clutch Erin's hand, and we form a clumsy chain as he leads us out of the woods and to his truck, parked beside Erin's Jeep.

He lets the tailgate down and motions for us to take a seat, and then he disappears into the restaurant.

"Maybe we should make a run for it," Jena suggests.

"Ha! Taeli isn't going anywhere. Not with Graham Tuttle fawning over her," Erin quips.

"He is not fawning over me," I snap.

"You like him," Jena says.

All of their eyes come to me.

"He's okay," I admit.

"Okay?" Jena gasps.

"Yeah, I guess. What?"

"Sure, the bossy but sweet, successful, handsome man that you were making swoony eyes at is okay," Erin states.

"I did not swoon," I deny.

"Ansley?" Erin turns to the other girl and raises an eyebrow.

Ansley leans around her and looks at me. "Sorry, Tae. You totally swooned."

"Well, it's rude to point it out." I huff.

"Shh, here he comes," Jena whisper-shouts.

Chapter
twelve

Graham

I HAVE THE FOUR OF THEM SITTING ON THE TAILGATE OF MY TRUCK, wrapped up in blankets from my roadside emergency kit, when Ted's truck pulls into the parking lot.

He parks and hops out. Shaking his head at the sight of the shivering women.

"What the hell happened?" he asks the group at large.

All four of them start talking at once. We get that they were having dinner. Something about a round of shots being bought by a group of cute guys and a trout with a diamond pearl.

Ted looks at me and shrugs. "Did that make sense to you?" he asks.

"Nope."

He turns back to them, and they all start talking again.

He raises his hand to stop them.

"You, go," he says, pointing at Ansley.

Erin starts to speak, and he stops her, indicating that he wants Ansley to start first.

"We were just having dinner and a few beers when Erin noticed that Taeli was wearing her wedding rings, so we decided to do a ring toss," Ansley begins, and Ted lowers his eyes to the ground and starts shaking his head.

"And, well, it was good and all. Taeli took them off and tossed them far away into the creek. Then, we were celebrating when she told us how much they were worth, and we kind of freaked out and jumped in to find them, but it was dark, and the water was moving fast. We finally gave up, and that's when Graham found us."

Ted looks up at me. "These crazy-ass women."

I chuckle.

He turns back to them. "I expect this from you two"—he points at Erin and Jena—"but, Ansley, I expect you to be the voice of reason."

Ansley huffs. "Hey, a ring toss was in order."

"Whatever. Let's get you loony birds home," he says.

"You can take those three. I'll take Taeli up to Leona's on my way home. I'll drive by and get Erin in the morning for work and pick her car up. I talked to the owner, and it'll be fine here for the night," I tell him.

"Thanks, man. Come on, girls," he says as he corrals them into his Jeep.

Taeli stands and waves as they drive off while I shut the tailgate. I walk her around to the passenger side and help her in.

Once we are on the road, she lays her head against the window and goes quiet.

"So, Senior Day?" I ask to break the silence as we turn onto the road leading up the mountain.

"I kind of stole a patrol car and took it for a joyride through the valley," she explains.

I look over at her.

"That was you?" I ask, surprised. I was in college when Garrett graduated, but the story of the girl who stole Deputy Wyatt's patrol car reached me and Langford. We were impressed.

She sighs. "Yeah, that was me. My mom came down to the jail-house to get me. She was mad as a hornet. Screaming at me about how I could ruin my chances of getting into UT. I swear, Deputy Wyatt let me slide without charges just to get Leona Tilson out of his office. That and to pretend it hadn't happened because he was so embarrassed, but the genie was already out of that bottle."

"I can't believe that was you," I muse.

"I was wild as the wind once," she mutters.

I slide my eyes to her and reach over to pull a piece of driftwood from her hair.

"I think there is still a bit of that wild woman in you," I tell her.

That makes her smile.

"You threw your rings in the river," I say to prove my point.

She nods. "Yep. I didn't even realize I was still wearing them. That's how numb I am," she explains.

"Numb?"

"Not angry, not sad, not hurt. Just numb. It's weird. I'd rather feel anything, even the bad stuff, than nothing at all," she mutters.

"Believe it or not, that's when you know you've started to heal," I inform her.

"What?"

"The opposite of love isn't hate. It's indifference. So, if you weren't even mad enough to notice you were still wearing his rings, then you probably aren't in love anymore. It took me a long time to take my ring off. I did it when I realized I wasn't in love anymore," I confess.

"You stopped loving her?"

I look over at her.

"Mom told me about your wife. About what happened."

"No. I will love her forever. But to be in love is to be in each other's space, sharing a life. She's gone. Moved on to another place. I still love her and the life we shared, but my heart has been released to fall in love again. It took me a long time to understand that," I explain.

"Oh."

"So, hear this: You're not numb, Taeli. You're free, and it's okay to let go. Just try not to drown in the river in the middle of the night while you do so."

"I can't make any promises," she teases.

I pull up in front of her mother's house, and she opens the door to get out. I put the truck in park and hop out to follow and make sure she gets in safely.

She fumbles around with the potted plant under the bay window until she emerges with a key in hand.

Then, she tries to get it into the lock. It takes a couple of goes before she is successful, but I don't intervene. I just watch as she concentrates, curses, closes one eye, and repeats.

Before she can pull the door all the way, it flings open, and Leona is standing there in her housecoat and slippers.

"What in the world happened to you?" she asks Taeli as she takes her daughter in from top to toe.

"I fell in the creek," Taeli says as she pushes past her.

Leona turns and watches her as she goes, and then she looks back at me.

"Fell in the creek?" she asks.

I shrug. "That's where I found her and the girls," I say.

She bursts out into a fit of laughter.

Once she has her wits about her, she says, "I guess they had a good time."

"Yeah, I believe they did," I agree.

"Good. She needed to blow off some steam before she combusted," Leona muses.

Taeli's head pops back out of the door.

"You want any coffee or tea?" she asks, and then she looks at her mother. "Do we have tea?"

"Of course we have tea. This is the South."

Taeli's expectant gaze returns to me. "We have tea," she states.

"I think I'd better head on back home. I've got to be on a work site early in the morning."

Her brow furrows. "Oh, right. It's late. I'd better go to bed. Caleb will be up soon, and I have a job now," she says and then just walks back inside.

Leona laughs again. "Thank you for bringing her home, Graham."

"You're welcome. I didn't mind at all."

"I bet you didn't," she mutters under her breath.

"What was that?" I ask.

She waves me off. "Oh, nothing. You be safe and get on home, but you will be by tomorrow, won't you?" she asks.

"For what?"

"I think I want to expand the front porch to the side of the house. I'll need you to come and give me an estimate," she says.

"You just decided that this minute?"

The woman can think of a million things she wants to do to this old house just to get me out here when all she truly has to do is ask.

"I did."

"Yes, ma'am. I'll be by tomorrow."

"Perfect. Good night, Graham."

"Good night, Leona."

She walks inside and shuts and locks the door behind her, and I get in my truck and head home.

What a strange night.

Chapter
thirteen

Taeli

MY HEAD IS POUNDING. I CAN'T BELIEVE I'M HUNGOVER. I haven't had a hangover in a decade or longer. This is what I get for going out on a work night.

I drag myself into the office and find Erin seated behind her desk, looking none the worse for wear.

"Good morning, sunshine," she chirps as I drop my purse on my desk.

"How are you so chipper this morning? You drank more than I did last night," I grumble.

"Practice. That and the fact that Ted was so put out that I had to pull out the reserve sex last night to smooth things over. It was a work-out, and I'm pretty sure I sweated out most of the beer."

Reserve sex?

She reads my confused expression and explains, "You know, the sex you reserve for birthdays, anniversaries, and apologies."

I shake my head.

"The kinky stuff. Haven't you ever made an insane purchase, and instead of asking permission, you give him a blow job in the truck on the way home from his aunt Katherine's after she notices you are wearing new diamond earrings and decided to compliment them in front of everyone?"

"That's extremely specific," I point out, and she shrugs.

"Anyway, I've been dying for you to arrive. Tell me everything about the drive home," she says as she parks herself on the edge of my desk.

"There's nothing to tell. We just talked."

"About what?"

"Life," I admit.

She frowns. "You were soaking wet and in one of the town's hunkiest bachelor's trucks, alone, and all you did was talk?"

"I'm sorry to disappoint you."

She sighs. "It's fine. I'm sure you'll have another opportunity to ravage him," she says before hopping down and walking back to her desk.

"Who is ravaging who?" Sara-Beth asks as she makes her way in from the back of the office.

"No one," I answer before Erin can open her mouth.

I give her a stern look from across the room. She knew Graham's mother was back there.

Sara-Beth looks between the two of us and grins.

"You know, I was young once too," she tells us.

"I didn't see your car outside," I say.

"Hilton dropped me off. He's taking mine in for a tire rotation and oil change. He'll be back soon to help us pull all the decorations out."

"Decorations?" I ask.

"Yes. Independence Day is next week, and we have to get everything ready for the parade and fireworks."

It's almost July? I can't believe we've been here for three weeks already. Time flies.

106

Corbin, Weston, Morris, and Graham all show up to help Hilton set up the Fourth of July decor. They wrap every tree with red, white, and blue lights, hang flags in front of every campsite, and line the fencing with Americana buntings.

Once they finish here, they move on to help the town hang lighted stars from every lamppost in the valley and add festive adornment to the town hall and the fairgrounds.

Sara-Beth and I take several trips to the rental cabins to add a little patriotic pizzazz to them as well.

Balsam Ridge is proud of its country and its veterans. Independence Day is a big affair. The valley streets will be lined with tents, selling refreshments and sparklers, and everyone will set up their outdoor chairs to watch the massive fireworks display that is shot off from the festival grounds.

There won't be a single vacancy in town. The motels, campgrounds, and cabins are booked out for months ahead.

I'm excited for Caleb to experience the festivities for the first time. I loved them when I was little.

When we make it back to the office, I find my phone sitting on my desk, showing six missed calls. All from Damon.

Great. I guess I can't avoid him forever.

I tell Erin I'll be right back and excuse myself. I walk outside to return his calls.

I dial his number, and he answers on the second ring. Which is unusual. Being a doctor, he's not that easy to get ahold of. I talked to his voice mail more than I ever talked to him.

"Taeli," he answers.

"Hello, Damon. I saw you called. I'm assuming it's about the divorce filing."

"I got the papers. I haven't signed them yet, but I received them."

I figured as much.

"So, what do you need?" I ask.

"The practice is closed next week, and I want to see if Caleb wants to join me in Cabo. I thought we could rent a yacht."

I snicker at his request. "You want to take Caleb to Mexico?"

"Yes. Or you both could come if you're uncomfortable with that."

Is he serious?

"Yeah, no. I don't think I want to be stuck on a boat with you and your pregnant girlfriend for a week."

"Ivy isn't going."

"Why not?"

"She's too far along in her pregnancy. Her doctor advised against air travel, and I agree."

"So, you figured, *Why not ask my ex-wife to come along instead?* Rather than … I don't know … stay in Chicago with the woman who's about to have your baby!"

"She's not going to deliver next week."

"Oh, well, in that case …"

"Taeli, I miss you, and I miss my son. Is that so hard to believe?"

"Of course not, but I'm not flying off on vacation with you."

"Please," he begs.

"No, Damon. We're getting divorced. That means no more holidays, no more vacations, and no more family dinners together. You have a new family now."

"I'm sorry," he blurts out.

"Sorry for what exactly?"

"If I made you feel like you weren't enough. It was me. I knew I wasn't enough for you. You're perfect. The perfect wife and the perfect mother, and I just wanted someone who needed me. Someone who looked at me and treated me like I was a prize."

"That's the most deplorable excuse for cheating I've ever heard."

"It's the truth."

"I hope you got your wish and Ivy treats you like a god," I bite out.

"I'm sure you do."

"I'm being honest, Damon. Because I hate to think that you tore our family apart for nothing."

"Taeli …" There is so much anguish in the way he says that one word.

"Good-bye, Damon."

"What about Caleb?" he asks before I can click off the line.

"I'll talk to him tonight. If he wants to join you, I won't stop him."

"Tell him I'll FaceTime him tomorrow."

I end the call.

What are you doing, Damon?

He has a lot of nerve, trying to weasel his way back into my life. I guess his plaything is out of commission at the moment, so he figures I'll jump at the chance to spend a week on a yacht with him.

How pathetic does he think I am?

Hilton's truck pulls into the lot, and Graham and his brothers climb out.

"You guys all done?" I ask.

"Yep, we're heading back to work. Pop was just dropping us back to our vehicles," Weston answers.

Graham breaks off from the group and walks over to me.

"Is something wrong?" he asks, reading my thoughts.

I wave the phone in the air. "Just dealing with a nuisance."

He nods.

"What are your plans for the evening?" he asks.

I shrug.

"I don't know, but whatever they are, they are going to include Caleb."

"Would the two of you want to go listen to some live music?" he asks.

"I'm not taking my twelve-year-old into a bar."

"Of course not, I was talking about the band performing at the Blackbird Motel. They have a big cookout on the third Thursday of every month, and they showcase local artists and musicians. Garrett's old bandmates are playing tonight. It's completely kid-friendly."

"Oh, that sounds nice," I say.

"I can pick you guys up around six," he offers.

"Can Mom come too? I feel like I owe her after the last few nights. I don't want to leave her to eat alone."

"Sure."

"Okay. We'll see you at six."

"It's a date."

Chapter
fourteen

Graham

"So, you've got the hots for Leona's daughter," Corbin states. When I don't respond, he continues, "Not that I blame you. She's smoking. Mom told me about her no-good husband. What a dumbass he is. He had that at home, and he still went catting around? That assistant of his must have an enchanted—"

"Don't finish that sentence," I bark.

He throws his hands in the air. "Just sayin'."

I shake my head.

"So, what's your play?" he asks.

"What do you mean, my play?"

"She's just here for the summer, right? You planning on having a sexy fling?"

"I don't know," I answer honestly.

He grins. "I like this. I haven't seen you bent about a woman in ages. I bet Mom and Leona are stoked."

"There is nothing to be stoked about. We're friends."

"If you say so, brother."

"You're one to talk. I haven't heard you mention Susanna in a while."

Susanna is his on-again, off-again girlfriend.

He brings his hand up and rubs his forehead with his index finger and thumb. He's stressed. It's his tell.

"We're on a break right now," he says.

"Again?" I ask.

"You know she's crazy as hell."

Of course I do. The whole town knows that, but he loves her anyway.

"Is there anything I can do?" I ask.

"Don't tell Mom and Pop. They'll figure it out when I show up on the Fourth alone."

"My lips are sealed."

"Thanks, bro, and, hey, keep me informed on your sexy fling."

I pull up to Valley Fire and Rescue and let him out.

"See you at the picnic," he calls before he enters the building.

As soon as he disappears through the door, I grab my phone to text Langford.

Heads up. Corbin and Susanna broke up again.

I don't even get out of the parking lot before my phone dings with his response.

Fucking great. I'll go by and check in on him tonight.

We're all used to dealing with the fallout when Susanna decides to take off, and it's a pain in the ass, but all four of us are there to keep our brother from losing his shit.

Taeli calls and tells me that she is taking a renter out to show them two of the properties and is running late. I offer to pick Caleb and Leona up, so she can meet us at the Blackbird when she's done.

She calls her mom and texts me that she and Caleb will be ready by six and that she will meet us as soon as she can.

When I get to Leona's, she wrangles Caleb into the truck, and the three of us head into town.

Leona asks if we can stop at Market Square, so she can pick up an order from One with the Moon.

While she is in the boutique, Caleb and I walk the square.

We make our way into the Penny-Pinching Pack Rat. It's a thrift shop, tucked between the more upscale shops.

"Let's pop in here. I want to introduce you to someone," I tell him.

The bell on the door chimes as we walk inside, and an older gentleman with a limp comes shuffling out of the back. His coveralls and wiry gray beard give off the impression that he could be found in the woods, checking on an old moonshine still.

Zemry Wells. A war hero. A sourpuss and my pop's closest friend. I adore him.

"Who do you have here?" he asks when he catches sight of Caleb.

"Hi, Zemry. This is Caleb, Leona's grandson. Caleb, this is Zemry Wells," I introduce.

He looks at Caleb and grunts. "You like boiled peanuts, boy?"

"What?" Caleb asks and looks up at me.

"Did I stutter?" Zemry asks.

"No, sir," Caleb says.

"Well, do you?"

"I don't know what that is," Caleb admits.

"It's peanuts that are boiled. Pretty self-explanatory, don't you think?"

"I guess."

"Come on," Zemry says and motions for Caleb to follow him deeper into the store.

I nudge him forward, and Caleb apprehensively falls in step behind him.

Zemry leads him over to two large steel pots resting over a coal stove. He opens the top of one of the pots, ladles a huge scoop of peanuts into a Styrofoam cup, and hands it to Caleb.

"These are the regular boil since you're a beginner, but I'm famous for my Cajun recipe," he tells him before preparing a cup of the spicy version for me.

Caleb watches as I take one of the nuts and crack the shell. I suck the juice from the pod and then slurp the tender nuts into my mouth.

I moan as the delicacy touches my tongue. Nothing reminds me of childhood like Zemry's boiled peanuts.

"Your turn," Zemry says to Caleb.

We watch as he mimics me. He wrinkles his nose as he chews and swallows.

"Well?" Zemry asks.

"It's salty and slimy," Caleb says.

"That's how it's supposed to be," Zemry assures him.

Caleb tries another.

"They'll grow on you," Zemry states.

We kill time, meandering around the shop, looking at the old antiques. Caleb is fascinated by some of the Native American tools and old knives.

"Here," Zemry says as he hands Caleb a tarnished pocketknife with a carved ivory handle.

"I don't have any money," Caleb tells him.

"It's a gift. You don't pay for gifts."

"I'm not sure my mom will let me have it," Caleb says as he looks up at me.

"Every boy needs a pocketknife. If Taeli or Leona has a problem with it, you send them to me, and I'll sort them," Zemry says.

"Thank you," Caleb offers.

Zemry just grunts and shuffles off. Caleb's eyes follow him, and then his head snaps to me.

"It's him. Isn't it?" he asks excitedly.

"It's who?"

"The *one old grump*, like the sign says. Mom said I'd know when I saw him. It's Zemry. He's the town's old grump!"

I laugh. "Yep, it's Zemry."

Leona finds us as we exit, and the three of us decide to leave the truck and walk three blocks to the Blackbird Motel. Caleb tells her about the pocketknife, and she makes him give it up until he asks his mother for permission to carry it.

I expect the kid to pitch a fit, but he doesn't. He just hands it over.

"I didn't think it was okay for me to keep it," he tells her.

"I can keep it safe until she decides it's time for you to have it."

We find a crosswalk and make our way across the street. When we arrive, Taeli is already waiting for us at the entrance.

"Mom, I met the grump!" Caleb tells her.

"You did?"

"Yep, and he yelled at us and made me eat slimy peanuts."

Her eyes come to me as she fights back a laugh.

"That does sound grumpy," she tells him.

"I think he's secretly nice, but he doesn't want anyone to know it. He even gave me a knife."

"He did what?"

"Don't worry. I gave it to Granna. She's going to put it up until I'm bigger."

"Okay," Taeli says as she looks between us.

I walk over and open the door. "Shall we?"

The three of them file in. I lead them through the lobby to the door that opens to the courtyard. I pay our entrance fee, which covers the food and compensation for the band. Leona chooses our seats at a picnic table close to the stage.

We enjoy an evening of burgers and tunes. Leona dances with an older gentleman in attendance and then tries to teach Caleb how to shag as he cackles.

I can't take my eyes off Taeli, who is alight, watching her boy and his grandmother.

Her glow is so bright, the moon is jealous.

Chapter
fifteen

Graham

CALEB STARTS TO GET TIRED, AND LEONA ASKS TO TAKE HIM HOME in Taeli's car.

"I'll take you. That way, Graham doesn't have to drive to the farm," Taeli insists.

"You act as if he lives across the county. He lives fifteen minutes down the road from me," Leona presses.

"That's half an hour round trip," Taeli tells her.

"Graham paid for us all to enjoy the music. You two stay out as long as you want. Caleb and I are tired. We're just going to go climb into our pajamas and go to sleep."

Taeli starts to argue, but Leona cuts her off.

"You don't mind bringing her home, do you, Graham?"

"No, ma'am."

"It's settled, then. We'll see you in the morning," she says as she holds out her hand for the keys.

Taeli gives in and fishes her keys out of her purse.

"Be careful," she pleads as she embraces Caleb and kisses her mother's cheek.

"I always am," she assures her daughter.

I leave Taeli at the table and walk Leona and Caleb to the Volvo parked in front of the motel. When I return, she has a companion sitting beside her. He stops mid-conversation and looks up at me as I approach.

"Graham," he greets.

It's Boyd Jackson, a guy who went to school with me and Langford.

"Good to see you, Boyd."

I look at Taeli, whose eyes are begging me to help her.

"You need another drink, Taeli?" I ask.

"I'd love one," she answers.

Boyd's gaze drifts between the two of us. Then, he excuses himself and moves on to the next table, occupied by a single female.

"I leave you alone for five minutes, and the vultures start circling," I say as I settle in beside her.

"Thank you for the rescue."

"You're quite welcome," I say as I flag our waitress down.

The band takes the stage after their short break. I find her hand resting on her knee under the table and thread our fingers together. She doesn't resist. Instead, she scoots closer to me and leans into my side. We sit wordlessly and enjoy the music until the last song is played.

I introduce her to the band after the show ends, and we say our good-byes to everyone before I lead her down the sidewalk the few blocks to my truck.

She yawns as I help her into the passenger seat, and by the time I pull on the street, she is already nodding off.

I try to take it easy, so I don't disturb her, but as soon as my tires hit gravel, her eyes blink open. She lays her head against the back of the bench and curls her legs up into the seat. I throw my right arm around her shoulders and tug her across the leather until she is settled against me. She wraps an arm across my waist and snuggles into my side.

"Thanks for inviting us tonight. It's great, seeing Caleb enjoying himself," she says.

"He's a good kid," I tell her.

"He's addicted to electronics and being angry with his mother," she states.

I chuckle.

"He didn't seem angry tonight," I point out.

"There's always tomorrow."

I cut off the lights as we roll up to the house. The house is dark, except for a single candle in the window Leona must have lit for Taeli.

She doesn't move from me when I turn off the engine.

We sit in silence for a while until she speaks.

"I can't remember when I had a better day—or month really," she confesses.

"I see you're starting to like being home."

"Yeah, it's been eye-opening."

"In what way?" I ask.

"I realize that I was pushing my way to the next step in life and checking off these boxes I'd made for myself. Marry an ambitious man. Check. Open your own business. Check. Build the dream house in the dream neighborhood. Check. Join the club and make fabulous friends. Check. Have two-point-five kids and get them into a private school. Half a check."

"Sounds like you were achieving your dreams," I say.

"That's just it. I was achieving them but not living them. I was just checking off boxes," she admits.

"And now?"

"And now, I have no idea what comes next. I don't have any boxes because the whole damn list was set on fire, but the funny thing is, I'm enjoying not knowing what's next. I like working at the rental company and coming in and having Erin there every day. I'm learning who my mother is instead of assuming who she is. I watched her dance with my son tonight. It was magical."

"Sounds like you needed a reminder of how to enjoy the simple things in life, and the universe gave you one," I tell her.

"You think the universe could have been a little bit gentler with that reminder?" she says.

I laugh. "It doesn't always work like that. Big changes are sometimes painful and can be scary as hell, but honestly, the most beautiful things in life usually start as scary changes."

"So, here's to hoping for more fright in our life," she deadpans.

"Something like that."

Speaking of scary things ...

I look down into her beautiful face and lay a soft kiss on her nose. She sighs, and her eyes flutter shut. Then, I kiss the corner of her cheek and the corner of her mouth.

When her eyes open again, there is heat in her gaze.

I dip my head again and take her mouth. This kiss is different than the ones we shared before. This kiss is claiming. I let go of the hesitation and let myself feel this unexplainable attraction I have to her.

She doesn't resist. She opens for me and kisses me back with a desperate passion.

I feel like a teenager, making out with my prom date in the cab of my truck. When you are all hands and mouths and raging hormones. I haven't felt this consuming fire for a woman in so long.

I know she feels it, too, when she climbs onto my lap and straddles me.

I pull her close, and the weight of her body against me does nothing to extinguish the flame. It only causes my body to combust.

She rakes her teeth over my bottom lip before capturing my tongue and sucking it into her mouth. She continues to suck on it until my hips jump off the seat of the truck, which causes her to jolt forward and against the steering wheel.

The horn is engaged, and a loud, long noise blares into the silent night. Startling us both and causing the front light to blink on and the door to the farmhouse to fly open.

Fuck.

"Busted," she says as her forehead falls against my chest.

My hard-on is throbbing against my jeans as she lifts herself to move to the passenger side again.

I groan.

"Sorry," she apologizes.

"I'm the sorry one. I should have taken you to my house for a nightcap like a grown-up instead of trying to ravage you in my truck like a horny teenager," I say.

She looks at me and grins. "I thought I was ravaging you," she teases.

I lean over and place another quick kiss on her lips. "You can ravage me anytime."

The porch light goes off, and her eyes widen.

"I'd better go inside in case the horn woke Caleb," she whispers.

"Before you go, I want another date. I want to take you to that winery Leona mentioned the other day. Would you be up for it?"

"I think I can do that," she says.

"Okay, good. It's a date. I'll see you tomorrow," I tell her before kissing her one more time.

"Good night, Graham."

She grabs the door handle and jumps out quickly, like she had to force herself to hurry out before she changed her mind.

I turn the headlights on and watch her. She turns one last time and waves before she disappears behind the door.

Damn, she's beautiful, and I'm in trouble.

Chapter
sixteen

Graham

I WENT HOME LAST NIGHT AND TOOK A LONG, COLD SHOWER. THEN, I lay awake, thinking about Taeli all night. I wasn't lying when I said changes are scary, but anything worth doing or having is worth it.

I spend the morning on a jobsite. We are clearing trees and prepping the land at the top of one of the mountain peaks for an old gold mine–themed amusement park, complete with roller coasters and other rides along with an old Western town full of saloons and bank robbers, cowboys, and gunslingers. It's every little boy's dream. A major investor took on the project, and it's being overseen by the company that manages Dollywood in Sevierville. The valley is excited about the tourism that it will draw along with the ski resort that Langford is helping to open next winter.

After overseeing the beginning of the excavation, I head down to Mom's office to pick up some contracts that Pop had his attorneys look over for me.

I check my messages when I get a phone signal and find out some auto parts I've been anxiously waiting for have come in, and I decide to call it an early day.

I walk into the office and catch the end of a tense moment between Taeli and her son.

"Whatever," Caleb snaps before putting in his earbuds and walking away from her desk.

She gives me an apologetic look when she catches my eye.

"Hi, Graham," she greets.

"Hey. Rough afternoon?" I ask.

She slides her eyes across the room to where he has plopped down in a chair.

"He hates me," she says.

"No, he doesn't," I disagree.

She brings her eyes to me. "Oh, yes, he does. He told me so this morning."

I chuckle. "Every kid says that at one time or another. If they don't, you aren't parenting right. You aren't supposed to be his friend. You're his mother."

"Can't I be both?" she asks.

"Eventually, like when he's a grown man, but not now. The worst thing for a teenager is to have a friend instead of a mother."

Her concerned eyes flicker to him again.

"I hope you're right," she mutters.

Then, she looks back at me, shakes her head, and snaps back into professional mode.

"I'm sorry. Sara-Beth said you were dropping in. I'll get those contracts for you," she says and walks off down the hallway.

I look over and see her son sitting in a chair in the corner of the small office with his head buried in a device.

I stroll to him and look over his shoulder at the screen to see he is engrossed in a computer game.

When he realizes someone is in his space, he peeks up at me through his bangs that have settled over his eyes.

"Hi," I say.

"Hi, Graham," he replies.

I stand up and lean against the wall at his side.

"I'm going to the soda shop for a burger, and then I'm going to pick up some parts that came in at the post office and head to my garage to work on my Firebird for a bit. You interested?" I ask him.

His brows furrow. "Interested in what?" he asks.

I shrug. "In having a burger and helping me work on my car," I reply.

"You want me to help you? I don't know how to work on cars," he says.

"I can teach you. It's gotta be more fun than sitting here all afternoon, fiddling with that thing." I nod to the gadget he is grasping.

He looks down at the game and then up to the clock above his mother's desk. Then, his eyes come back to me.

"I am hungry," he admits, and I know I have him.

I call out to Taeli, and she comes from the file room and looks at me standing here with Caleb.

"Do you mind if I steal Caleb here for the afternoon?"

She glances down at her son.

"We're going to eat burgers and work on cars," he tells her.

Surprise washes over her as she brings her gaze back to me.

"I'm going to show him how to replace the alternator and the spark plugs on a 1977 Pontiac Firebird Trans Am."

"You still have that car?" she asks.

"I sure do. It's in the garage at my office on blocks while I wait for some parts to come in. How did you know about it?"

"Garrett used to drive it sometimes when we were in school. The girls, including me, would drool over it."

Yeah, my brother was always begging to use it when I was away at college.

"Can I go, Mom?" Caleb asks.

She grins and then looks to her son and gives in. "Okay. You leave your phone and tablet here and listen to Mr. Tuttle," she instructs.

He hands over the device, and she fishes in her wallet for cash and hands it to him. He takes the money and shoves it into his pocket.

"I'll be right back," he says before taking off for the bathroom.

Taeli watches him and then turns to me. "I'll come by to get him once I'm done here. Around five thirty."

"That'll be fine," I agree.

"Thank you," she says, and I can hear the relief in her voice.

"No problem. It'll be fun to have a helper," I assure her.

"Yeah, and anything that keeps him off this for a few hours is great," she says as she waves the gadget in the air.

I grab a pen off her desk and scribble my office address on the corner of her desk calendar. "You'll find us here," I tell her.

"I'll be there as soon as I can."

"See you then," I say before Caleb rejoins us, and I walk out of the office with him right behind me.

"Hand me the wrench sitting on top of the toolbox," I instruct.

Caleb does as asked, and I loosen and remove the bolts holding the old alternator in place.

"Open your hands," I tell him.

He does, and I drop the bolts in his palms.

"Hold on to those. We'll need them to attach the new one."

He nods enthusiastically.

"Have you ever worked on a car before?" I ask as I pull the old part out and set it aside.

"Nope."

"Ever driven a car?" I ask.

"I'm only twelve," he informs me.

"I know, but my dad let me drive around the yard when I was your age."

His eyes go wide. "He did?"

"Yep. He was right there beside me, but he wanted me to be comfortable behind the wheel before I turned fifteen and could start driver's ed."

"I wish my dad had time to teach me stuff like that," he admits.

"I reckon doctors are pretty busy guys, huh?" I ask.

"Yeah. He mainly just hires tutors when I need help, or Mom teaches me what she can, but she's a girl."

"Sounds like you're a lucky guy to have a mom like that."

"I guess so," he responds.

"You don't think your mom's that great?"

He shrugs.

"What's your problem with her? You tell me, and I'll keep it just between us. Man to man."

I can tell he likes the idea of being talked to like a man as he considers spilling.

"She doesn't ask me," he says.

"Doesn't ask you what?"

"Anything. She just tells me. Like when we came here, she didn't ask me if I wanted to come to Tennessee. She just packed my stuff and told me we were visiting Granna for the whole summer."

"And you don't like it here?"

"No. I want to go back. I miss my friends, and I like our house. It's big—really big. My room is three times as big as Uncle Gene's room, and we have a pool," he explains.

"A pool, huh?"

"Yeah, and a game room, and the television is huge."

"But you have a whole river in your backyard now," I point out.

"I know. It's just Granna's house is old and small, and there aren't any neighbors," he grumbles.

"You know, Caleb, you can build a house out of cow dung or solid gold. Both keep you just as warm and dry. Bigger doesn't mean better. All that matters is whether or not it's filled with love and if you're happy."

"What if smaller doesn't make me happy?"

"It takes a lot of work to be happy, son. Happiness doesn't just fall out of the sky. A man has to make his happy."

He wrinkles his nose.

I lay down my tools and wipe my greasy hands with a towel. "Take today, for example. Did you have fun?"

"Sure."

"You like working on the old car, huh?"

He nods.

"Maybe you're meant to be a mechanic. Or a mechanical engineer."

"My dad wants me to be a doctor, like him," he tells me.

"That's a good job too. If it makes you happy. Whatever you decide to do, work hard. Don't do anything half-ass, whether it's medical school or trade school. Respect is earned from the quality of work you put out, not the title in front of your name or the size of your house," I say.

He ponders that for a moment.

"And, Caleb, respect and show up for your mom. No matter what you think she did or didn't do. Showing up is what real men do, and that's what everyone is going to remember about you. Don't be like your uncle Gene. Not a soul in this town would spit on him if he was on fire because of the way he abandoned your grandmother in her time of need."

"I won't ever leave my mom," he says.

I ruffle his hair. "Give her some grace about coming here. She's been through a lot these past few months, and she's trying her best."

"I know."

"Now, let's get this motor put back together and take this machine for a joyride through the valley," I suggest.

"Yeah," he agrees.

We cruise up and down the valley a few times when I decide to pull into the festival grounds. The space is an eight-acre venue, fully equipped with water and electricity, internet connection, restrooms, concession stands, a large stage, and an ample parking lot. It's home to many classic car and Jeep shows, motorcycle rallies, craft fairs, holiday markets, an autumn concert series, and much more, but today, it is empty.

I pull into the center of the grounds and park. I take the keys from the ignition and hand them to Caleb.

He looks from the keys to me.

"What are we doing?" he asks.

"I'm going to give you your first driving lesson."

His eyes go wide. "What?"

"Switch places with me," I say as I open my door and exit the car.

He does as I asked, and he climbs behind the steering wheel and me in the passenger seat.

He is so nervous that he white-knuckles the steering wheel before I even get settled beside him.

"Are you ready?" I ask.

He shakes his head. "What if I crash it?" he asks.

"That's why I brought you here. There's no traffic. No lines to stay in. It's just a big, open field. You aren't going to hit anything or anyone. We'll just go over the basics."

He relaxes a little, and I show him how to adjust his seat and mirrors and give him an overview of the controls.

When he is comfortable and ready, he slides the key into the ignition. A huge smile spreads across his face as the engine roars to life.

For the next few hours, he gets used to driving, uses the signal to make right and left turns, and backs up in a straight line. We end with a few head-spinning doughnuts, and the kid has a blast.

I'm fairly sure he didn't miss his video games for a second.

Chapter
seventeen

Taeli

WHEN I PICK CALEB UP FROM GRAHAM'S WORKPLACE, HE IS like a completely different kid. He is glowing, and I don't get two steps from my vehicle before he starts chattering away about his day.

"Wait, you did what?" I ask.

"I drove the Trans Am! It was so cool, Mom!" he cries.

I look at Graham, confused.

"I took him to the festival grounds and let him drive it around for a while. It was all safe," he assures me.

I'm not completely convinced letting my twelve-year-old behind the wheel of an expensive classic car was a good idea, but the excitement in Caleb's voice is so beautiful to hear that I bite back my concern.

"I'm a great backer-upper," he proudly declares.

"Backer-upper, huh?"

"Yeah, Graham says I'm a natural. I could do it in a straight line after only three tries. He said it took him a long time to master a straight line," he babbles.

Pride fills me as my little man brags on himself.

This. This is the kind of thing he should be doing instead of staying on a tablet all day.

I look up to Graham and mouth the words, *Thank you,* and he winks at me.

"Are you ready to go back to Granna's? I'm sure Graham would like to get home himself."

He looks over to Graham and grins, and then he brings his eyes back to me.

"We want to make you dinner," he says.

"We who?" I ask.

"Graham and me. We want to make you dinner at Graham's house."

I bend down and look him in the eyes. "Since when do you cook?" I ask.

"I don't. Yet. But I learned how to drive today, so I figure cooking can't be that hard."

"Well, you're just full of surprises, aren't you?" I say as I tug a piece of his hair from his eyes.

He nods.

I stand and look at Graham. "Are you sure about this? Or did the kid here talk you into it?" I ask.

"It was all my idea. I agreed to keep Langford's boy tonight. He and Caleb are close to the same age. The three of us will cook you the best meal you've ever had," he swears.

"Okay. Let's see what kind of culinary skills you guys have."

I call Mom to let her know of our dinner plans. Instead of sounding put out, she sounds thrilled with the idea.

We follow Graham to his house, and Langford is there, dropping his son, Tucker, off. Graham introduces us, and Tucker looks back and forth between us.

"Is she your girlfriend, Uncle Graham?" Tucker asks.

Caleb's eyes go round, and he looks between us with curious eyes.

Graham clears his throat.

"We're friends," he says at the same time Caleb says, "No, she's married to my dad."

Tucker shrugs and looks at Caleb. "Race you to the backyard?"

He takes off running, and Caleb immediately sprints off after him.

"He thinks we'll get back together, like before," I utter.

"Even with the new baby on the way?" Graham asks.

"We haven't told him yet," I admit.

Graham looks confused. "Isn't he or she due in a couple of months?"

"Yeah, next month."

"Don't you think you should tell him before he comes home to a sibling one day?" he asks.

"I just didn't want to ruin his summer any worse than I already have," I admit.

"He's more mature than you realize, Taeli. I think he can handle it. I'm not saying he'll like it, but I think he deserves the truth."

"I know. I was hoping Damon would have the conversation with him, but I'm going to tell him soon."

He wraps an arm around my shoulders and guides me toward the house.

"How do you feel about bacon?" he asks, changing the subject.

"Bacon?"

"Yes."

"Totally pro-bacon over here," I answer.

"Good."

We walk inside of his home, and my mouth drops open. It's as stunning inside as it is outside. I walk to the living room and to the large glass wall that overlooks the mountain. The view is breathtaking.

"I would stare out this window all the time," I tell him.

He comes up behind me. "I do a lot of that. It never gets old."

"I bet not."

"Would you like a glass of wine?" he asks.

I nod, and he leads me over to the massive kitchen.

There is a set of sliding glass doors that lead from the kitchen out onto a deck with a built-in gas grill, a griddle top, and a charcoal pizza oven.

Impressive.

I can see the boys skipping stones in the small stream tucked behind the house.

They're talking up a storm and laughing.

Graham opens a bottle of red and hands me a glass.

Then, he opens one of the doors and calls to the boys, "Chef Graham needs his sous-chefs to come wash up."

They drop the rocks they were holding and come running.

I watch as they wash their hands. Graham starts grabbing supplies from the large stainless steel refrigerator and instructs the boys to gather what they need from the pantry.

I offer my assistance, but Caleb banishes me to the living room, so they can cook for me.

I sit on the plush, large sofa and enjoy the view of the three of them moving around in the kitchen.

Graham is patient with them and lets them help with every detail of the meal, except for the grilling of the steaks themselves. They chop up vegetables for a salad and fry bacon and shred a block of cheddar for the twice-baked potatoes. He even teaches them how to make an Italian apple cider vinegar dressing from scratch.

When the food is ready, they set places for us out on the deck and proudly escort me to my seat. Tucker pours us all glasses of water, and Caleb helps Graham load our plates. He sets mine in front of me with a look of overwhelming pride.

"Thank you so much, buddy. This looks delicious," I praise.

He grins at me and stands there, patiently waiting as I pour dressing over my salad and take the first bite.

"Mmm," I moan.

His eyes light up, and he hurries over to the seat beside Tucker.

We take our time eating the tasty meal and talk about everything from soccer to fishing to the next time they will cook together as the sun sets behind the mountain.

The boys discuss the Independence Day picnic and parade.

Tucker tells Caleb how amazing the fireworks display is in the valley and invites us to park with them in his church parking lot because it's the best viewing spot in town.

It's a lovely evening, and my heart is full and grateful as I watch my son make a new friend.

Chapter
eighteen

Taeli

AFTER WE FINISH EATING, THE BOYS HAVE NO PROBLEM LETTING me help Graham clean up while they take off downstairs to the game room to shoot a game on the red-top pool table.

Once we're done, we curl up on the couch with our glasses of wine.

Tucker comes bouncing up the stairs and eyes the two of us. We are facing each other, and Graham's hand is resting on my knee. He quickly pulls it back when we hear Tucker enter the room.

"Lame," Tucker says as he shakes his head.

"What?" Graham asks.

"Seriously, Uncle Graham? You have no game," the kid teases.

Graham straightens his back. "I have game. I have an entire Sunday lineup of game," he protests.

"Keep telling yourself that," Tucker says as he heads to the kitchen to grab sodas before running back down to the game room.

I burst into laughter as the door shuts behind him.

Graham's amused eyes come to me. "You think I have game, right?"

"Oh, yes," I say.

He pulls me into him for a kiss, and I think to myself, *He doesn't need game. He just has to be himself.*

We make out on the couch until my lips are bruised and he is so worked up that he looks like he is in pain. He stands to answer the knock at the door an hour later.

Langford comes in and smirks at us as Graham calls down to let Tucker know that his dad is here to pick him up.

"I take it, you guys had a good time?" Langford asks when his son and Caleb appear.

"We did. We made the best supper ever for Taeli. Steaks and cheesy potatoes and salad," Tucker tells his dad.

He looks at Graham and grins. "I bet I know what you had for dessert."

Tucker's brows furrow. "We didn't make dessert," he says, confused.

Langford laughs and tousles his son's hair.

"Are you ready to head home?" he asks Tucker.

"Can Caleb spend the night? I want to show him my fishing gear. He wants to learn how to fly-fish," Tucker asks.

"He does?" I ask.

Caleb looks over at me. "Yeah. Tucker says we can catch trout and make you dinner again with the food we catch with our own hands. How cool is that?"

"Very cool," I answer.

"Please, Dad, can he stay over?" Tucker asks again.

Langford looks at me. "It's okay with me if it's okay with you."

"He doesn't have any of his things," I begin.

Langford cuts me off. "They're boys and about the same age. I'm sure I have an extra toothbrush, and Tucker can find a pair of pajamas.

Besides, you two might want to finish dessert," he says as he looks at Graham.

Graham gives his older brother a look that says, *Shut the hell up*.

"I want dessert," Caleb quips.

"We can stop at the Dairy Barn for ice cream on the way home. If your mom lets you go," Langford tells him.

"Please, Mom," Caleb pleads.

"Okay. You be good and mind Tucker's dad," I instruct, and he promises he will.

The boys get their shoes on, and we follow them to the door.

"I can pick him up first thing in the morning, or you can drop him off to me at the office later if you'd like," I tell Langford as they make their way out to his truck.

"I'll call you. I have a light schedule. I might take them fishing."

"Yay!" the boys holler at the news.

"All right. See you tomorrow. I love you," I call to Caleb, and he just waves as he follows Tucker.

We watch as they pull off, and then Graham turns to me.

"About that dessert ..."

He doesn't even get the words out of his mouth and the door shut behind us before I throw myself into his arms.

We continue our make-out session on the couch until he suggests that we have a sleepover ourselves.

I call Mom to tell her that we will be out all night, and she doesn't even question me as to why. She just tells me to enjoy my night.

"I don't have an overnight bag either. Do you have an extra toothbrush and pajamas I can sleep in?" I ask Graham.

He shakes his head.

"Oh well. Guess I'll have to sleep naked, then," I say as I walk off toward his bedroom.

I remove my shirt and toss it on the bed as I make my way to his bathroom, where I pull off my jeans and underwear and let them fall to the floor.

I turn on the shower without looking back for him, and I step into the warm spray.

I don't turn around as I hear him enter the bathroom.

He stands there for a while, just watching me as I take the shampoo and lather it in my hair.

"Are you coming in?" I ask over my shoulder.

The shower door opens and closes.

Finally, I feel his heat at my back. Then his lips on my ear.

I lean my head back onto his chest, and I blink up at him as the soap rinses out of my hair and slides down our bodies.

He reaches up and runs his fingers through my long locks, and it feels so damn good.

I grasp the knob and slowly turn it, and the spray gradually gets warmer.

"What are you doing?" he asks as he moves my hair and touches his lips to my shoulder.

I open my eyes to a cloud of steam licking its way up the shower door.

His hands rest on my hips as he pulls me back into him. He slides his hands around my stomach as he begins to gently suck at my throat.

A whimper escapes me as his hands continue to explore my bare skin.

He strokes the underside of my breasts before taking their weight into his palms. My knees grow weak as the pads of his thumbs begin to circle my sensitive nipples.

"Graham," I moan his name as I sink further into him.

"Does that feel good, baby?" he asks as he rolls the tender peaks between his fingers.

"Yes, ah."

He wedges one of his knees between my legs to steady me, and the contact sends a shudder through me.

I reach out to the tiles for support and bear down on him to get better pressure where I want it. A needy sound rises in my throat, and then all of a sudden, Graham picks me up and spins me around. My back hits the shower wall, and his mouth covers mine.

His control finally snaps, and his kiss grows wild. His teeth sink into my bottom lip, and I gasp. He takes the opportunity to hungrily suck my tongue into his mouth. I feed my arms around his neck and tug at his wet hair. I can't get him close enough.

He tears his mouth from mine, and the passion in his eyes sears me as they move down my body like a physical touch. His hands begin kneading my swollen breasts again, and I lean my head back. His mouth finds the curve of my neck and kisses a trail down my collarbone. I close my eyes and just feel as his teeth graze one of my nipples. I throw my arms out wide and brace myself on the wall. He sucks it into his mouth and begins to pull gently at the other. Heat pools in my belly as one of his hands moves up the inside of my thigh.

I cry out at his touch when his fingertips find my swollen entrance.

His mouth releases my nipple, and his head comes up to look at my face as I tremble. His forehead comes to mine as he sinks a finger inside of me.

"Taeli," he half-breathes and half-moans my name.

I grab his shoulders as he adds a second finger.

"So hot," he murmurs as he brings his head to my shoulder and gently bites into my flesh.

"Please," I beg as I dig my nails into his skin.

I need more. More of him.

"I want to taste you," he says as he pulls away and then goes to a knee.

He kisses a path from my breast down to my stomach as he continues to pump his fingers in and out of me at a maddening pace.

When his mouth reaches his fingers, he spreads me open, and his tongue circles my entrance. A jolt of electricity climbs up my spine as he sucks my clit deep.

He slips one of my legs over his shoulder to give himself better access, and he holds me steady against the shower wall before he buries his face in my warmth and starts to lap at me like a starving man. I grab handfuls of his hair and hold him where I want him. Where I need him.

His tongue finds my opening, and he begins to thrust in and out of me. I bring my hips up and start moving to meet him. My hands in his hair tighten as I hold him in place, and I ride his tongue. I'm so close. He pinches my clit, and I fall over the edge.

One minute, I am screaming his name as I come, and the next, I'm being lifted and hoisted up and out of the shower. He carries me into his room and drops me to my feet, turning me to face the dresser. I grasp the edge of the wood and hold on as he pulls my hips back and pushes a knee between my legs. My knees fall apart, opening me wide to him.

"So damn beautiful," he says as his eyes meet mine in the mirror.

I watch as he takes his cock into his hand and brings the tip to my entrance.

I close my eyes as he slides it through my folds, coating it in my wetness. Then, he releases it and grabs the side of the dresser, enveloping me before pushing into me fully from behind.

I groan and then whisper, "You feel so good inside of me."

It's like my words flip a switch. He lets out a growl and grabs my hips. Then, he pulls out and buries himself back inside me. I rise on my toes to meet his thrusts as his rhythm quickens. I know my body is climbing, and I want more. More of his mouth on me, more of his skin against mine, just more of him.

My legs start to shake uncontrollably as I come undone. I can tell he's holding on by a thread as my body ignites and I begin to spasm around him. He closes his eyes, and his head flies back as he pumps his release inside of me.

Once we both come down, he brings his eyes to mine in the mirror. Still inside of me, he leans in and kisses the spot where he bit me tenderly before he slides out.

"Don't move," he whispers against my skin.

He disappears into the bathroom and returns a moment later with a large towel that he uses to dry my back. I turn, and he wraps it around my shoulders.

Suddenly, he lifts me in his arms without saying a word and walks me to the bed and lays me down. He covers me with the soft comforter and tucks me in, and then he lies down beside me and snuggles close.

I fall asleep, wrapped in his strong arms, and it's the best sleep I've had in a long time.

Chapter
nineteen

Taeli

I WALK INTO THE HOUSE, TRYING TO BE AS QUIET AS POSSIBLE. SARA-Beth's car is in the drive, and I don't want to face her and Mom and their questions about my sleepover with her son.

I tiptoe to the stairs when I hear the sound of music and high-pitched squealing coming from the back deck. Curiosity gets the best of me, and I follow the beat.

I find them on the screened porch, prancing around in leg warmers and headbands.

"Mom? Sara-Beth? What are you doing?" I ask.

"Dancing our way to a svelte figure," Sara-Beth answers.

"Is that an old Richard Simmons video?" I ask as I enter the room and catch a glimpse of his shiny bootie shorts.

"Yes, it's *Sweatin' to the Oldies*. We love it," Mom says as she pants.

"How are you playing that thing? It has to be ancient," I ask as I search for the VCR.

"Morris took my VHS tape and loaded it onto one of those DVDs for us," Sara-Beth says.

"And it's not ancient. It's a classic, and it's fun!" Mom adds.

They continue to shake their booties.

"Are you wearing a leotard?" I ask Mom.

"What else should I work out in?"

I shake my head.

"You should join us," Sara-Beth suggests.

"I can't. I have to get to work. I don't want to upset my boss by running late."

Richard calls out for them to do a cooldown. Mom hands Sara-Beth a towel, and they dry off.

"Did you have fun last night?" Mom asks me.

"Yeah. I'm sorry about missing dinner," I tell her.

She waves me off. "Don't worry about it. I had a hot date myself," she says.

She what?

"You had a date? With who?" I ask.

"My old beau, Ralph."

"Mr. Gentry? The mayor?" I screech.

Mom and our town's mayor dated when they were teenagers before she met my father and fell madly in love.

"That's the one," she confirms.

"What happened to Mrs. Gentry?"

"She died about five years ago. Heart attack," Sara-Beth informs me.

"I can't believe you're dating," I tell Mom.

"There hasn't been a curtain call on my life yet. It's in the third act. It's my choice whether or not this act is going to be a grand finale or a tragic ending," she says.

"But what about Daddy?"

"What about him?" she asks.

"I guess I just never thought about you ever being with someone else."

"Oh, sweetheart, I'll always miss your father. He was the love of my life, but I didn't stop living when he did. I had to figure out what my life would look like, going forward. Life after being Bernard Tilson's wife," she says.

"Life after wife. Sounds like the title to a cheesy self-help book," I mumble.

"Or a second-chance romance," Sara-Beth adds.

Mom walks over to me and places her hands on my cheeks. "It might sound cheesy, but it's true, and the same goes for you. You don't have to be a prisoner to who you were. It wasn't a jail sentence; it was a marriage. You're allowed to have a life after wife too, you know."

"It feels weird," I whisper.

"What does?" she asks.

"Being happy or excited when I should be upset," I admit.

"Oh, Taeli, there is nothing wrong with moving on."

"I feel like I don't deserve to. I couldn't keep my marriage together."

"Don't do that, Taeli. Don't play the martyr. You're not a puddle. People stomp through puddles. You, my dear, are a mighty river," she scolds.

When did she become so inspirational?

"Play? You think I'm playing, Mom? This is my life."

"Yeah, well, life happens to all of us. There isn't a person alive who doesn't have a sad story to tell. It's up to each person to decide whether they're going to be the hero or the victim of their own story. So, what are you going to be?" she asks.

I look between her and Sara-Beth, who is listening intently.

"You make it sound so simple with your dancing and yoga and remodeling. But I'm dealing with a lot of shit right now," I tell her.

"So?"

"So?!"

"Shitty things have happened to you. Your life isn't shit. Take a look around. Shitty things have happened to us all. I lost your father. One day, he was here, and the next, he was gone. There was no fight. No anger. Just a kiss good-bye, and off we went about our day. Throw a rock, and anyone it hits is dealing with something shitty. You could trade with them, but guess what. Shit is shit. It's just different shit, is all," she says.

"Can you stop saying shit?" I ask.

"Shit, shit, shit," she chants.

Sara-Beth starts to giggle, and before I know it, all three of us are laughing out loud.

"You're right," I tell her once I catch my breath.

"I know. I'm old, so being wise is what I do," she says.

"Mayor Gentry, huh?"

"He's a silver fox, and he likes my cookies," she says.

"I bet he likes your cookies," Sara-Beth mutters.

"Okay, I'm out," I say before excusing myself and running upstairs to get ready for the day.

Mom calls up after me, "The cookies might be mature, but they're still tasty!"

"I can't hear you," I yell from the landing.

Their laughter floats up.

Crazy old ladies.

I walk in the office door ten minutes late.

"Crap, I'm sorry I'm late. It's Mom and Sara-Beth's fault, I swear," I tell Erin as I come barreling through the door.

"It's fine," she says.

I sit down and turn on my laptop when she speaks again.

"Your cell phone is in your top drawer."

"My what?" I ask as I slide open the drawer to see my phone is indeed tucked inside.

"Yeah, Graham came by. He said you left it at his house, and he didn't want you to panic when you realized you didn't have it."

"Oh," I say.

"Oh, nothing. Spill," she demands.

"There's nothing to 'spill," I tell her.

"Girl, you are covered in a morning afterglow, so don't even try. I'm calling Jena and Ansley. We're having a lunch meeting," she says before picking up the phone to dial.

"A lunch meeting?" I ask.

"Yep, and you are going to tell us everything."

I get up, run over to her desk, and grab the phone. "No, you don't. I don't need any rumors started. I've already had to deal with my reputation being ruined in one town."

She huffs. "First of all, Jena, Ansley and I would never start rumors. What are we, sixteen? Besides, reputations are just history passed down the gossip train. You can change them anytime you want to."

"You don't care what people think about you?" I surmise.

"Nope, and neither should you," she points out. "Besides, why is getting your freak on with a hot single man anything to be embarrassed about?" she asks.

"I'm not embarrassed. I just have to be careful because of Caleb," I tell her.

"Then it's a good thing Jena nor Ansley have your boy on speed dial. Now, give me back my phone and get ready to share all the tawdry details."

She holds her hand out, and I set the phone in her palm.

"Fine. Lunch meeting it is," I surrender.

I'm dying to tell someone anyway.

Chapter
twenty

Taeli

"OH MY," ERIN SAYS WHILE FANNING HERSELF.

"Yeah, I think I need a cigarette," Jena agrees.

"You don't smoke. Do you?" I ask.

She grins. "No, but I might start after that story."

"Right? I thought I was going to combust," Ansley agrees.

"Damn, girl, you're in town what, a month and a half, and you already snagged Graham Tuttle? I'm so impressed," Erin adds.

"I haven't snagged anyone. For all I know, it was a one-time thing. A really hot one-time thing."

Jena reaches over the table and places her hand on top of mine. "However long it lasts, let yourself enjoy it. After all you've been through, you deserve to be giddy over a new romance. It could be the beginning of your happily ever after or just a spicy anecdote before you move on to the next amore. Either way, it's what you need to recover."

"An anecdote is all it can be. I'm only on vacation. When I

return to my regularly scheduled life, he won't be a part of it," I tell them.

"Unless you decide to stay," Ansley says.

"I can't do that."

"Sure you can. You can do anything you want to do, and we'd love for you to stick around. Our threesome could use a fourth," Jena points out.

A warmth slides down my spine.

It's nice to feel wanted.

"Now, tell us more about your mom and Mayor Gentry," Erin requests.

"I thought you guys weren't ones to start rumors?" I ask her.

"It's not a rumor if it's true," she replies.

I place my head in my hands. "I can't believe my mom has a boyfriend. You guys, I never imagined it," I cry.

"Why not? She's still a woman. He's a dapper bachelor. I say, good for them both. If anything happens to Ted, I pray I can find another man to spin me around the dance floor."

"Me too," Jena agrees.

"And Mayor Gentry is a great catch. His children and grandchildren adore him, as does the entire town. You couldn't ask for a better man for your mom to spend her time with," Erin says.

Ansley nods.

"I like him. He's just not my daddy," I mutter.

"I'm sure he's not trying to be. He just likes Leona. That's a good thing," she insists.

"There is a reason our wedding vows say *until death do us part*. God doesn't want or expect us to be alone after he calls our spouse home. He wants us to be free to find love again," Ansley explains.

"I'd take him for a stepdad," Erin adds.

I let their words sink in and realize they're right. I do want that for my mother. Just like I hope Caleb wants that for me one day. Her finding love with another man doesn't take a single moment of love away from her and Daddy.

"I know you're right. I'll do my best to accept it and support Mom."

"Atta girl," Ansley says.

"Thanks, guys. I needed this," I tell them.

"Anytime. That's what friends are for," Jena says.

It's strange. I never had this level of intimacy with the women I called friends back home in Illinois. The lunches were plentiful but the support and honesty were null, and I didn't recognize it for the farce it was. True, deep friendship means so much more. It's sharing the good, bad, and ugly and loving each other through it all.

After lunch, Erin and I head back to the office. Langford shows up with the boys around four, and they are a bundle of excitement.

"Mom, I caught a fish!" Caleb howls.

"You did?"

"Yeah, it was a big one. Tucker and his dad caught a whole bunch, but mine was the biggest one," he says proudly.

Langford walks over and places a hand on Caleb's shoulder. "It was the biggest and very impressive for his first time with a fly rod."

"We're going to have it for dinner," Caleb announces.

"You are?" I ask.

"Yeah, Tucker's grandpa is going to get the guts out."

I grimace, and Caleb and Tucker giggle.

I lift my eyes to Langford.

"Pop is cleaning the fish. The boys want to camp in a tent with him tonight and have an old-fashioned fish fry."

"Can I, Mom?" Caleb asks.

"Please," Tucker adds to the pleading.

I can't believe my son is standing before me begging to go camping.

"If it's okay with Hilton, it's okay with me," I tell them, and the boys cheer before scurrying out of the office to find Hilton.

"Thank you for taking him along with you guys today," I tell Langford.

"The boys had a ball. He's welcome to fish with us anytime," he assures me.

He leaves to help the boys set up the campsite, and I call Mom to ask her to bring Caleb an overnight bag.

When she arrives, I have her fetch my son, and the three of us have a sit-down in the break room.

"Caleb, I need to talk to you about next week," I start.

He smiles.

"Your dad called, and he wants to know if you'd like to go to Cabo with him."

He wrinkles his forehead. "What about the picnic and fireworks?" he asks.

"You'd have to miss those."

"Are you going to come to the beach?" he asks.

"No, buddy. It would just be you and Dad."

He frowns.

"We've never gone anywhere by ourselves before," he states.

It's true. Other than an occasional father and son golf outing with friends, Damon never spent one-on-one time with Caleb. It was always the three of us.

"I know, but it could be fun. Just the two of you. You could show him your new fishing skills," I encourage.

I can see the indecision in his eyes.

"I wanted to watch the fireworks with Tucker and Chris," he mumbles.

I was looking forward to watching them with him as well, but

I don't let the disappointment show. I know this decision is hard enough for him to make.

"It's up to you. You don't have to go, but if you do want to go with your dad, I promise that we'll have a picnic and shoot some fireworks of our own at the farm when you get back, and we'll invite your friends," Mom tells him.

"So, Dad will bring me back here?"

"Of course he will," I assure him.

He sighs. "Okay, I'll go with Dad," he says with a hint of sadness.

It sucks to watch him struggle between letting his father down and staying to enjoy something new with the friends he's made. What a mess we've made of his life.

"Can I go back to the tent now?" he asks.

"Yes. I'll call your dad and get everything set up. You go enjoy your night."

He hurries out the door, and I slump in my chair.

"It will be okay," Mom tells me.

"I know. It just sucks," I tell her as I take my phone and text Damon, saying Caleb wants to join him on vacation and ask him to fly into Knoxville so I can bring Caleb to meet him at the airport.

"Do you have plans tonight?" Mom asks.

"I don't."

"Do you want to spend the evening with your mother?" she asks.

"Sure. What do you have in mind?" I ask.

"I was thinking of having a baking party. I'll call Sara-Beth, and you can invite your new friends," she suggests.

"I'm in," Erin calls from her desk.

"Wonderful. Tell the other girls," Mom shouts.

"On it," Erin replies.

"I guess it's a date," I tell Mom.

She stands. "I'll head to the market and get all the supplies. We'll have wine and a charcuterie tray and get all the baking we need to get done for the Independence Day picnic."

"Aha! You're using us as slave labor," I muse.

"I'm providing you with wine and snacks—that's compensation," she says as she heads to the door.

She stops at Erin's desk. "The more, the merrier. Seven o'clock."

"We'll be there," Erin confirms.

Chapter
twenty-one

Taeli

MOM HAS A SPREAD FIT FOR A LIFESTYLE MAGAZINE ON THE dining room table when Erin and I arrive.

Jena and Ansley are already in the kitchen, chatting with Mom and Sara-Beth.

"You're here! Grab a glass. You two have some catching up to do," Mom squeals as we enter the room.

Erin pours us each a glass of red wine, and I walk over to the stove to see a pot of greens boiling.

"I thought we were baking. What are the greens for?" I ask.

Mom looks over her shoulder at me. "Those aren't greens. That's weed. I'm making cannabutter," she says.

"Canna what?"

"Cannabutter. I use it to make my medicinal candies and brownies," she explains.

Dear Lord.

"I didn't realize we were going to be running drugs at the Fourth of July picnic," I muse.

"It's not for the picnic. It's for my personal consumption and a few gift baskets," she clarifies.

"Okay, but if we get busted, you're taking the fall," I tease.

We take our time filling our stomachs and chatting before Mom supplies us all with red or blue aprons and puts us to work.

"Taeli, you start the sugar cookie dough," she instructs.

"As long as there is no herbal-enhanced butter involved," I say.

She starts loading the island with everything I need—butter, sugar, flour, et cetera.

"You could use some herbal enhancement, if you ask me. But we'll keep this batch PG," she replies.

Erin and Ansley are assigned blondies, Jena gets royal-icing duty, and Mom and Sara-Beth tackle cupcakes.

We spend the next hour mixing ingredients and kneading dough. I use the cookie cutters to cut out the perfect festive patterns—stars, flags, patriotic top hats, and hearts.

We place them in the double oven and pour ourselves more wine. I leave the girls at the table, chatting and picking over the food that's left, and join Mom and Sara-Beth out on the porch while the cookies and cakes bake.

I sit in the rocker and look out over the yard. The old fort that Daddy built for Gene and me in one of the trees is still standing. The rope ladder swaying in the breeze. It's the same yet different. No cows are mooing in the distance, and no horses are grazing inside the fence line.

"I'm sorry I wasn't here for you when Dad died," I say as I look over to Mom.

She smiles at me. "Oh, honey, you had a life. I didn't expect you to stop living for me," she says.

"I should have. Our relationship was always contentious when I was growing up, but I should have been here when you needed me."

Like she has been here for me.

"You might have been able to keep the farm," I add.

She laughs. "Oh, kiddo, I had no desire to keep the farm going. That was your father's passion, and he wanted to leave something for Gene."

"I can't believe he just left you like he did."

She shrugs. "He wanted to live his own life too. I suspect he only stayed around here because he didn't want to disappoint your father. Running a farm for the rest of his life was never his dream."

"It must have been hard when he took off."

"At first, I tried to keep up with everything, and it was scary. Then, I realized I didn't have to. I called Sara-Beth, and she sent Hilton and Graham out here to survey the land. They helped me parcel it off into four five-acre lots. They found buyers for the live-stock. I kept the parcel with the house, my gardens, and barn, and they put the other three on the market. They sold within two weeks. I still have my home, my view of the mountains, all the pri-vacy I need, and the sale gave me a very nice nest egg to live off of."

"I'm glad you had them," I say as I reach for Sara-Beth's hand on the rocker beside me and squeeze. "I just … it was hard to come back here," I admit.

"That's because you were a daddy's girl," Mom surmises.

I think about that for a minute, and it's true. My daddy was my rock. The one I could always count on. I thought he was the only one.

"It took losing him for me to see you," I confess.

"I know, and it's okay," she tells me.

"It's not," I whisper.

Before I can say more, the timer goes off on the stove. We stand, and I follow them back inside.

I look down at the cookies and remove the ones that have expanded and cracked. I set them aside. I place the others on a cooling rack, so I can add the icing Jena colored red, white, and blue.

"What are you doing with those?" Mom asks.

"Throwing them out. They're messed up," I answer.

She reaches into the cupboard and hands me a sugar shaker. "Here, just sprinkle them with powdered sugar. They don't have to be perfect. The beauty of the cookie is in the imperfections," she says.

"It is?" I ask.

"Oh, yes, look at them. They taste the same as the others. They came from the same batch of dough. So they have cracks. Big deal. It gives them character and they'll still be just as delicious."

I look up at her. "Are you trying to tell me something, Mom?"

"I'm telling you, you don't waste good cookies because they don't meet your idea or expectation of perfection. You throw some sparkle on them and take them to enjoy the party."

All righty then.

She and Sara-Beth start adding food coloring to the buttercream icing they prepared and scoop it into bags.

"Hey, Mom," I say, and she looks up at me. "I never realized that spending time with you could be so rad."

She smiles. "I knew spending time with you could be."

I pull up a music app on my phone and connect it to the Bluetooth speaker in the kitchen.

The six of us dance around the island, singing at the tops of our lungs, decorating our confections, and enjoying our time together.

By the time we are done, sweaty, and covered in flour and sugar, we have six dozen decorated cookies; eighteen tins of blondies with red-and-blue-coated candies; twelve dozen cupcakes with red, white, and blue sprinkles or sanding sugar; and of course, a large batch of Mom's special medicinal toffee.

I shoo the girls off to go home and leave the cleanup to Mom and me.

"It was a fun night," Jena says as she hugs me good-bye.

Erin and Ansley agree.

It truly was.

Once they are all on their way, Mom and I roll up our sleeves to clean the kitchen.

"That was a blast. I'm so glad you and the girls came to pitch in," Mom says.

I help her pile the dirty pans and glasses beside the sink and wet a cloth to wash down the island.

"We had a good time and they're great. It's like we've been friends forever."

"That's the way it is with true friends. It's like your souls connect from the beginning," she muses.

"They want me to stay here in Balsam Ridge. Can you believe that?"

"The better question is, can you see yourself living here again?"

"Don't talk in circles, Mom. I'm seeking your advice here," I say.

"You're a smart, beautiful, and capable woman. I'm not going to tell you what to do."

She fills the sink with warm water and starts to soak the dishes. I stop beside her.

"Since when?" I ask.

"Today."

"Come on, Mom. I know you have an opinion. What do you think I should do?"

She drops a stack of plates into the sink with a loud clank, picks up a sponge and starts to scrub them. "I think you should start concentrating on what *you* think instead of what everyone else does," she says.

"You've always wanted to control my life and my decisions, but now that I'm actually seeking a little motherly guidance, all of a sudden, you think I should make up my own mind?" I ask for clarification.

"I've never wanted to control your life, Taeli."

"Oh, come on, Mom. That's all you've ever done. When I was in high school, you were the only mother who went to every single away game and made me stay in the same room as you."

"After I caught you sneaking out of your bedroom window. It was a consequence of your actions, Taeli. I didn't want you to get into any trouble. It was my job to protect you," she insists.

"More like embarrass me," I grumble.

"Oh, please. You're just projecting. You aren't still angry about that stuff. It was years ago," she chides.

"I am still angry. I wish we could have had a better relationship, but you never got to know me in a way that we could be friends. All you ever did was ground me or scold me."

"Because I was your mother, not your girlfriend. A mother's love is many things. It's gentle, it's kind, it's stern, it's teaching and rearing, and yes, sometimes, it's punishing. But it is unconditional. The love that breastfed you, rocked you to sleep when you had colic, made you chocolate chip pancakes every Saturday morning, and kissed your skinned knees is the same love that whipped your behind when you needed it. Fierce, crazy, and at times, angry love. That's what I always gave to you. Always."

"Always? You didn't talk to me for almost two years when I followed Damon to Northwestern. The only communication I got from you was through Daddy, and I'm sure ninety percent of that was him pretending you cared."

She tosses the sponge she was using into the sink and turns to face me. "Pretending I cared? Taeli, I'm your mother. All I'm capable of doing is caring. Yes, I was upset when you left school and wasted your scholarship. I thought you were throwing away your future," she explains.

"Don't you think I know that now, Mom? Walking away from the full-ride education was the worst decision of my life, but I was young and blinded by love."

"Exactly. You were blinded, and I was trying to be the guiding light for you," she explains.

"I should have listened to you. There, I said it. Go ahead and say *I told you so*. You've been waiting so long."

She shakes her head. "No, kiddo, I wasn't. God had a different plan for you. I see that now. I was never meant to write your book. I was just the narrator for the first few chapters. I look at you today, and I see a lovely, strong, resilient woman, who I'm proud to call my daughter. A good mother. A better mother than I ever was. If you had listened to me, we wouldn't have Caleb. What would we do without him?" she says.

I sigh.

"Now, I'm ruining his life too."

"No, you're not. You're doing what needs to be done. Sometimes, being a good mother is defined by making the hard decisions. Don't stay buried under the weight of them. Caleb will understand. It may not be tomorrow, but one day he will," she assures.

"You think leaving was the right decision?" I ask.

"Yes, I do. You needed space and distance to sort yourself."

"Sort myself," I repeat.

"Exactly. You were dealt a raw deal. You were hurt and humiliated, but you don't have to stay hurt and humiliated and turn bitter. You can rise up like a phoenix from the ashes of that pain, and in the process of healing, you just might find that you feel more alive than you ever have. The door has been opened, baby girl. All you have to do is walk through it."

I let her words permeate my soul.

"You still talking to God?" I ask, breaking the tension.

She huffs. "Of course I am. Why do you sound so surprised?"

"I didn't realize the big guy was a fan of your extracurricular activities," I tease, trying to lighten the moment.

"Oh, don't be such an old fuddy-duddy. God doesn't mind me using my crops for healing. He makes it grow. I don't overindulge, and it's better than drinking myself numb," she defends.

I shrug. "If you say so," I muse.

"Listen, I settled it with the Lord, and that means it's settled. You and the other gossiping old biddies in town are just going to have to accept me for who I am," she declares.

She returns to washing dishes, and I step behind her and wrap my arms around her shoulders. I kiss her cheek.

"I can do that, Mom."

"And so can I," she whispers with a catch in her voice.

"I still don't know what to do."

"Well, kiddo, it's your life and your book. Now, all you have to do is turn the page, and you'll get to start a brand-new chapter."

"Yeah, I wonder who all will be in this story."

"Anyone. Everyone. Just make sure you choose what you want this time."

We end our night in her bed, watching a sappy movie and falling asleep side by side.

When I awake in the morning, I have a voice mail from Damon.

Asshole.

I take my phone upstairs and dial his number. I pace back and forth, growing angrier and angrier as it rings.

"Hello?"

"What the fuck, Damon?"

He sighs. "I know."

"No, you don't know. He is going to be so disappointed. Why did you even have me tell him you wanted him to go with you if you were going to cancel?" I ask.

"Something came up."

"Oh, really? What could be more important than seeing your son?"

"It's an emergency at the office."

I scoff.

"What?" he asks.

"Try again, Damon. You can't possibly know of an emergency that is going to take place next week." I call him out on his bullshit.

The line goes silent while he scrambles to come up with a better excuse.

"I should have known better. You decided not to go the minute I told you I wouldn't and you still let me ask Caleb and get his hopes up. You were counting on him to convince me to go too, weren't you?"

"That's not true."

"Liar. I don't know why I thought you might actually want to spend time with Caleb. You selfish bastard!" I scream.

"What about you?" he yells across the line.

Me?

"What about me?" I ask.

"Graham Tuttle," he spits out.

How does he know about him?

"What about Graham?"

"Is he that singer you went to school with? The one who comes from one of the wealthy families in Balsam Ridge," he asks.

"No, that's Garrett. Graham is his older brother and he has nothing to do with this."

"When I talked to Caleb, he told me that he drove your friend Graham's car."

"So?"

"He's twelve, Taeli. He shouldn't be driving anything."

"He was in an open field without any other cars. Graham was just letting him get a feel for it. It was completely safe. I was driving my daddy's truck around the farm when I was ten," I tell him.

"I should be the one teaching him to drive, not Graham fucking Tuttle," he roars.

"Then, why haven't you?" I ask.

"Because he's twelve."

"Name one thing you've taught him, Damon. I'll wait."

"I'm a good father," he growls.

"You're a good provider, Damon. That's it, but life is more than a big house and expensive sneakers. When was the last time you spent more than five minutes with him, having a real conversation?" I ask.

"I talk to him."

"I don't blame you. I'm just as at fault as you are. We let video games and television raise him while we built the practice, but I'm done with that. I'd rather live in a shack, wearing threadbare clothes, and know my kid than live in a mansion on a hill and him be a stranger."

"I have to go. Tell Caleb I'm sorry," he says.

"I'm not telling him. You—"

I don't get the sentence out before the line goes dead.

I flip on my bed and scream into my pillow.

I hate him.

Chapter
twenty-two

Graham

POP CALLED AND ROPED ME INTO A NIGHT OF CAMPING WITH Langford and the boys down by the creek, roasting fish over a campfire and telling ghost stories. Pop even had them draw water from the stream and showed them how to boil it over the open flames and let it cool for drinking.

"We'll teach you how to start a fire without the assistance of a match next time," Pop tells them.

"I already know how, Grandpa. They taught us in Boy Scouts," Tucker informs him.

"Then, you can show Caleb," Pop suggests.

Tucker looks to his new friend. "Do you have Boy Scouts up north?" he asks.

Caleb shrugs. "I don't know."

"Don't you go to summer camp?" Tucker asks.

Caleb nods. "Oh, yeah. I do summer soccer camp, and we do a golf camp at the club."

Tucker wrinkles his nose. "Golf camp? You like golf?"

"Not really. My dad does, and he makes me do it, so I can learn and play with his friends in father-son tournaments. It's really boring."

"Too bad you don't live here. You could join the Scouts with me. It's loads of fun. We go fishing, camping, and hiking. They teach us stuff, like how to pitch our own tents, build fires, clean fish, swim safety, cooking, rock climbing, archery, kayaking, and all sorts of cool things."

"Sounds fun," Caleb tells him.

"Don't worry. Dad, Uncle Graham, Grandpa, and I will teach you all we can before you leave," Tucker tells him.

"Thanks. I really like fishing. I want to catch a bunch next time to make dinner for Mom and Granna."

Not once the entire night does he ask for or even miss his phone or video games. It's the most carefree I've seen him since he arrived.

Pop leads the boys into the woods for a bathroom break, and Langford and I grab a beer from the cooler and sit by the fire.

"So, you and Taeli have fun last night?" he asks.

"We did."

He nods his head as he takes a pull on his bottle. "That's good."

"Thanks for offering to take the boys. I'll repay that gesture," I inform him.

"It was my pleasure. He's a good kid. A little quiet, but Tucker brought him around."

Just in time for them to leave town.

"So, are you and Taeli a thing now?" he asks.

Before I can answer, the boys come bounding back to the campsite.

"Time for s'mores," Pop announces.

When we awake in the morning, we eat a breakfast of scrambled eggs and bacon, cooked over the fire. Then, we all help tear down the tents and pack up.

I call Taeli to tell her I'll bring Caleb home, and we hop into my truck and head up the mountain.

He chatters the whole way home. It's a far cry from the closed-off kid he usually is. I think the mountains are working their magic on him.

When we make it to the farmhouse, I follow him inside. We end up in the kitchen, and he snatches a piece of toffee from a Tupperware container on the countertop.

Taeli comes down the hall when she hears us milling around.

"Don't eat that!" Taeli screams and swats the confection from his hand.

"Mom!" he shouts.

"That's not for kids. Granna made it, and it has marijuana in it. It will get you high and get social services called on me," she explains.

His eyes go wide. "Granna makes pot candy?" he asks.

She blinks. "You know what that is?" she asks him.

He rolls his eyes. "I'm not lame, Mom. I know what pot is. I thought you smoked it, not ate it," he replies.

"Have you ever smoked it?" she asks cautiously.

"No. I'm twelve. I don't want to stunt my growth," he says.

"And it's illegal and a bad idea, and it leads to other bad habits," she corrects him.

He turns to her and grins. "That too," he agrees.

Leona walks in from the back deck, and we all look to her.

"You make pot candy, Granna?" Caleb asks.

"I do. It's for my glaucoma," she says as she pinches his cheek.

"Glaucoma? I thought you said it was for your arthritis," Taeli asks.

"That too," Leona replies as she takes a piece and pops it into her mouth.

Caleb giggles.

"What? It's herbal medication," she insists.

"Yeah, and Mom's wine is a natural stress reliever," Caleb adds.

"Hey, I don't drink that often," Taeli defends.

"I know. And I've never seen Granna high. At least, I don't think so. She's always a little loopy," he whispers the last part.

Leona laughs.

"I'm a free spirit, remember? We're loopy loos," she says as she places a finger under his chin and lifts his face to hers. "Besides, I don't like chemical pharmaceuticals. Those are overprescribed and made to be addictive, causing an epidemic. God gave us the means to take care of ourselves naturally." She kisses him on his forehead and flutters past us.

Taeli's eyes meet mine, and she shakes her head.

"Good talk," she declares.

"Yep," Caleb agrees and then asks, "Are the cookies safe?"

She lets out a breath. "Yeah, have at them, kid."

He grabs a handful from one of the baskets and takes off up the stairs to his room.

Taeli's worried eyes follow him.

"Something wrong?" I ask.

She looks at me. "Yeah. Damon called the other day, trying to convince me to hop on a plane with Caleb and join him for a vacation in Cabo. Apparently, Ivy is too far along in the pregnancy to travel."

"What?" I ask a little louder than I meant to.

"I know. He's insane, and I told him so, but he asked about Caleb going, and I told him I'd give Caleb the option of accompanying him by himself. I thought it would do them both some good to spend quality father-son time together."

I nod my agreement. It's important that Caleb knows his father wants to see him and that what's happening with his parents has nothing to do with their love for him.

"Caleb didn't want to go?" I guess.

She shakes her head. "No. He agreed to go, so I texted Damon and told him to book his flight to come to Knoxville, and he and Caleb could go on to Cabo together from there."

"And?" I prompt her to continue.

"And this morning, I received a voice mail from him, telling me that something came up and he wasn't going to be able to make the trip. So I called him back. We argued and the asshole wants me to break the news to Caleb."

The coward.

I prop a hip against the island.

"So, he wanted to take you and Caleb, but once he realized you wouldn't be joining them, he bailed on his kid. What a jackass," I say.

"Right?! And now, I have to find a way to tell Caleb without calling his father a jackass because I don't want him to think of him that way."

"He's a smart kid. He'll figure that out for himself."

Pain passes over her face. "I don't want that for him. I don't want him to feel unwanted. Damon is just punishing me because I refused his invitation to join them."

I walk over and clasp her shoulders. "No, he's being a dick because he didn't get his way."

"And Caleb is the one who will suffer."

She plants her head on my chest, and I kiss the top of her head.

"I have an idea," I tell her.

She brings her hopeful eyes to mine.

"You want to go fishing?" I ask.

Chapter
twenty-three

Graham

"I CAN'T BELIEVE I LET YOU TWO TALK ME INTO THIS," TAELI SAYS as she walks out of the dressing room at the outfitter shop.

I whistle when she does a little twirl to show Caleb and me her chest-high waders.

"You like?" she asks.

"I do like," I tell her.

She'd look good in a potato sack.

Caleb giggles.

The salesgirl chimes in from behind us, "It's perfect. Waders and flannel are the latest in lady lumberjack fashion. They're the new little black dress of the valley."

Taeli looks at herself in the mirror. No makeup, hair pulled back in a ponytail, and a smile on her face.

She's absolutely stunning.

She catches my eye in the reflection, and her cheeks flush. I hold her stare, letting her know in no uncertain terms how gorgeous I think she is.

"Now what?" Caleb asks, breaking the moment.

I bend down to him and whisper, "Now, we find her some boots."

"Yeah!" He skips over and takes her by the hand. "Come on, Mom. Let's get you some real wading boots," he urges.

Taeli obliges and lets him lead her over to the boot section, and I follow.

Once we have her tricked out with her pants and footwear, I grab a bucket hat and a pair of ladies' wraparound, polarized sunglasses.

I walk over and tug the tie from her hair. She shakes her head, and her long locks fall across her shoulders and down her back. The scent of apples envelops me, and I breathe deep.

I pop the hat on her head and gently place the sunglasses on her face.

She grins. "I have sunglasses, you know."

I tug the hat further down on her forehead. "Those are for fashion. This bucket hat and these wraparound sunglasses, though they look awesome on you, are for safety. They keep the glare of the sun bouncing off the water out of your eyes. If your line breaks or gets caught in the wind and snaps back at you, you don't want to spend the night in the hospital, having a fly removed from your eye because you were blinded," I explain.

"No, there are definitely better ways to end our night than in a hospital," she agrees, and I step into her.

"Careful. My son is in the next aisle," she murmurs.

I slide my hands down to her ass and pull her in close. I lay a quick kiss on her nose.

"You started it," I accuse.

She comes up on her tiptoes and nips my earlobe with her teeth.

"And I'll finish it. Later," she whispers.

I growl just as Caleb rounds the rack a row over, holding a colorful dry fly.

"Can we get some of these? They're cool," he says.

Taeli quickly steps back and looks down at him. "Sure, buddy. What is it?"

"It's a fly. It's what we trick the fish with. They think it's a real fly, and they bite it."

"So, we don't have to put live worms on a hook?" she asks.

Caleb shakes his head. "Duh, it's called fly-fishing, silly."

We leave the outfitter shop and head down the creek bank. Caleb wades out into the water first, proud to show off his newfound skills to his mother.

He casts his line near the rocks upstream, which is a great technique.

"That was excellent, Caleb," I praise, and then I lead Taeli into the water beside him.

"See how his fly is hanging out in that cluster of rocks. That's a great place to concentrate on because trout hide in the rocks and wait for food to flow past them. You always fish upstream because it allows you to use the current to your advantage, the fish won't see you, and it's safer. Now, all Caleb has to do is wait for a tug on his line," I explain.

"Okay, I think I can do it," she says, and she takes her fly rod and whips it over her head before I can catch her.

"Whoa," I say as I watch her fly flop in the water about ten feet from Caleb's.

"You don't want to cross lines with him," I tell her just as Caleb cries, "Moooooom."

"Oh, sorry."

She steps back, pulling her rod with her. I come up behind her and take her hands in mine, helping her reel it back in.

Caleb looks over at us and rolls his eyes. "Girls," he says.

Taeli gasps and kicks at him, splashing water onto his waders.

"You're gonna scare the fish," he scolds.

She looks at me. "One afternoon fishing with your brother, and suddenly, he's an expert."

"He is a better student than you are," I say.

Her mouth falls open.

"It's true. Now, let's give you a lesson in casting, so you don't tangle with us or scare the trout."

It's a fun afternoon. Taeli never quite picks up the rhythm needed to be a good fisherwoman, but she tries, and Caleb has a great time, instructing her.

By the time dust settles over the mountain, he and I have bagged three nice-sized trout.

"Can we try one more cast? I want to catch another one, so Graham and I will be even," Caleb pleads.

"One more," Taeli agrees.

After we all get our lines in the water, I get her attention.

"Tell him now," I whisper.

She nods.

"Hey, bud," she calls.

"Yeah?"

"Remember that trip to Cabo with Dad?"

He nods.

"Well, he called this morning, and an emergency came up, so he won't be able to go now," she tells him.

He looks straight ahead and doesn't respond.

"Caleb, did you hear what I said?" she asks gently.

"Yep."

"Are you upset?" she asks.

Again, he doesn't respond.

"Do you want to talk about it?"

"No. It's fine. I'll just see him when we get home," he says, and the emotion is heavy in his voice.

Taeli cuts her eyes to me.

"At least you'll get to see the fireworks with Tucker now," she offers.

"Won't that be fun?" I ask, trying to help.

He looks over his shoulder at us. His brave face is firmly in place, but he is clearly disappointed.

He nods. "That's what I wanted to do. I should have told him no in the first place," he says.

The fact that he was more worried about hurting his father's feelings than his father was about hurting his makes me want to drive all night to Illinois to punch Damon in the face.

Caleb gets a tug at his line, and his head snaps around as he shouts, "I got one!"

I rush over to help him with his reel, and he is back to excitement when he pulls in the biggest catch of the day. He holds it up to proudly show his mother.

When he turns around, she mouths, *Thank you*, to me.

Being in the creek and having a good day softened the blow that I had known his father's cancellation would deliver.

I'm glad I was able to help.

We gather our gear and our catches and pile back into the truck. I take Taeli and Caleb to dinner in the valley before taking them home.

"I'll take the fish and put them on ice so that I can show you how to clean them tomorrow," I tell Caleb.

"Cool, I'm going to go find Granna," he says before hopping out and running inside to tell his grandmother about his day.

"You all right?" I ask Taeli.

"I'm all right as long as he is," she replies.

"He's lucky to have you," I tell her.

She shakes her head. "I'm the blessed one."

I lean over and kiss her temple.

"Will I see you tomorrow?" I ask.

She brings her eyes to mine. "Let me get Caleb to bed, and you can see me tonight," she says, "if you want to, that is."

I kiss her again. This time on the lips.

"Hurry. I'll be waiting for you."

She smiles and follows her son into the house.

I race home to unload before she arrives.

I get everything put away, shower, change into a pair of lounge pants, and build a fire before I hear her SUV pull into the drive.

I walk over to the door and swing it open before she has a chance to knock.

"Hi," she says.

She is wearing a linen dress, and her damp hair is pulled into a knot.

"I couldn't wait to get here, so I skipped drying my hair," she says.

Thank goodness.

I grab her around the waist and pull her inside.

She wraps her arms around my neck, and then we are all hands. I pull her hair loose and run my fingers through it as I walk her backward into the living room.

I maneuver her body around, sit down on the couch, and tug her onto my lap. She leans back on my thighs and concentrates on unbuttoning my shirt. Once it's open, her mouth finds my chest, and she runs her hands over my sides and around my back. She is soft and warm, pressed against me. I find her throat with my mouth, and she tastes so damn good. I let her explore my skin, and I can feel myself growing hard beneath her. She starts to slowly roll her hips against me, and I lay my head back against the couch and groan. The sound is deep and guttural, and she moans in response, letting me know that she wants this as badly as I do.

One second, her tongue is climbing the column of my throat as she writhes in my lap. The next second, I lace my hands under her ass and hoist her up as I stand to my feet.

"What are you doing?" she asks breathlessly.

"Taking you to bed," I growl as I head toward my room.

"What about the fire?" she asks.

"Let it burn," I mutter against her throat.

She giggles.

I hurry down the hallway and make a right into the master bedroom. I deposit her on the bed and quickly strip out of my slippers and lounge pants, tossing them on the floor before crawling up the bed and kissing her again.

She wraps her legs around my hips, the hem of her dress riding up to her waist. I'm hard and ready against the silk of her panties.

I take a finger and tug aside the plunging neckline of her dress, so my mouth can reach her breast.

As I take one taut nipple between my teeth and gently bite down, she cries out, "Graham!"

She plants her feet, raises her hips, and rocks them in a circle. Fuck yes, sweet contact. I don't think I've ever been this turned on before. My body is coiled tight and screaming for release.

I chuckle against her sensitive skin before lapping at her bud with my tongue.

"My impatient girl," I say as I sit upon my knees.

Her legs fall open for me.

I sit and reverently stare down at her. She's opening herself up to me completely.

I hook a finger into the sides of her panties and slowly slide them down her thighs.

She is totally exposed to me, so damn ready.

My finger glides through her glistening wetness before I come back on top of her.

189

She rakes her fingernails down my back as I find her entrance and slowly move inside.

Finally.

We keep a slow-building pace. My eyes never leave hers until my control snaps and I can no longer hold back. She locks her knees to my sides as my powerful hips move urgently. She rises to meet my thrusts as I increase my pace, chasing the burning sensation crawling up my spine. I hold on for as long as I can, and as soon as she begins to spasm around me, an explosion of pleasure sweeps me up. She scores her nails down my back, and I cover her mouth with mine to take her muffled cries until she is panting and sated.

I bury my face into her chest when I feel it vibrate.

I look up into her amused face.

"What?" I ask.

"I didn't even get my dress off," she points out.

I run my hand down her side and clutch the fabric.

"Let's start over, then," I say as I rise, taking her dress over her head and tossing it aside.

"Yes, please," she says before I cover her again and do just that.

Chapter
twenty-four

Taeli

I WAKE UP BEFORE GRAHAM, GET UP AS QUIETLY AS I CAN, AND MAKE my way to the bathroom.

I look a mess.

Grabbing my bag from the vanity, I dig around for my toothbrush and cosmetics.

I pull my hair into a ponytail and start applying moisturizer. Once my face is done, I take the tweezers and glue to add eyelashes. I misalign the one on the right and have to tug it loose. A speck of glue gets into my eye, causing me to yelp.

I blink repeatedly and swear like a sailor as I try to wink away the burn.

"Why do you women do that?"

Graham's sexy morning voice fills the room. I look up through my good eye to see him leaning against the doorframe. His hair is all over the place, and his dimples are dancing.

"Do what? Wear makeup?" I ask.

"No, glue those spider legs to your eyelids?"

I huff. "Because some of us can't grow luscious, long lashes," I inform him.

"Luscious?"

"Yeah, some are blessed, but the majority of us have to buy them."

"What a waste of money," he mutters.

"Excuse me?" I ask as I stare at him with one eye.

He leans in, places his hands on either side of me, and licks his lips.

"Let me tell you a secret, sweetheart. No man has ever looked at a woman and thought, *Damn, she's gorgeous, and I'd love to push her up against the wall and make her scream my name, if it wasn't for those short eyelashes she has.*"

Gooseflesh crawls down my arms as he starts to kiss my neck just below my ear.

Smartass.

"I have to go to work," I moan.

"So do I," he says against my pulse.

I stretch my neck to the side to give him better access to my throat.

"But I'm not my own boss. I have to be on time," I grumble.

"You will be," he says before picking me up and setting me on the vanity.

He steps between my legs, and I wrap them around his hips.

"I'm supposed to be there in twenty minutes," I inform him.

He kisses my lips and then says, "Okay, so maybe you'll be a few minutes late."

Thank goodness this is a temporary job.

I give in. "Okay, but you'll have to deal with my boss."

"I've got you," he says, and then he proceeds on making me more than a few minutes late.

194

It's a busy day at the office. Holiday weeks in a tourist town like Balsam Ridge are already a flurry of activity. Visitors from all over the country make their way to the valley to spend the week enjoying the festivities.

The campground is at maximum capacity, and I send at least a dozen travelers to other sites. Every motel in town is showing no vacancies available, and the rentals with Rocky Pass are all spoken for.

By the time I get into my vehicle to head home, I'm exhausted.

My phone rings, and I answer it without looking as I back out of the parking lot.

"Hello."

"Hi, sweetheart."

It's Damon.

Great.

"I'm not in the mood to talk, Damon," I bark in greeting.

"Long day?" he asks.

I don't answer.

"What do you want?" I ask.

"I had my attorney look over the divorce papers. I need to see you to talk about the terms you outlined."

"Just have your attorney contact mine," I suggest.

"No, I think you and I should work this out ourselves."

"There's nothing to work out. My proposal is more than fair."

"You want the house. I never agreed to that."

"It's Caleb's home."

"It's my home too," he insists.

"So, you don't care about the house. I designed it and picked out every detail. Now, all of a sudden, you want to keep it and make your son move?" I ask.

"That's not what I said."

"Well, someone has to move."

He sighs.

"Can't we just talk? I'll fly out there to you," he offers.

"That's not necessary."

"Taeli—"

"Just sign the damn papers, Damon!" I yell and then click off the line.

When I make it home, I find a note, letting me know that Mom and Weston took Caleb into town to pick up some supplies for the greenhouse and they will be back before dinner.

I look in the fridge to see Mom defrosted a roast, so I grab a tenderizing hammer and proceed to beat the crap out of the hunk of meat.

Then, I place it in the stove with potatoes and carrots. I chop vegetables for a salad and pulverize them to shreds.

"What the hell are you doing?" Mom asks as she walks into the kitchen with Weston and Caleb close behind.

"Rage cooking," I answer.

"I'm sorry, what?"

"Rage. Cooking. Now, sit down. All three of you. You're about to have the best meal of your life," I command.

Weston and Caleb hop onto stools at the island and watch in amusement as I continue to stomp around the kitchen.

When everything is done, I set a plate in front of them and plop down to eat myself.

Weston takes a bite and looks over at Mom.

"You should piss her off more often. This is amazing."

"I didn't piss her off," she says and then looks to me. "Did I?"

"No. It's just been a stressful day."

"Mom?" Caleb's tentative voice says.

I look over at my son and smile. "I'm okay, bud. Nothing some deep breathing and meditation won't cure."

Weston gives me a peculiar look. "Meditation? You're not one of those New Wave weirdos, are you?"

"Asks the man who supplies my mother with weed."

"Weed is not weird," he deadpans.

That makes me lose control and dissolve into a hoot of laughter.

"Mom. You're cuckoo," Caleb says.

"Why don't you run yourself a bath, and Caleb and I will clean up?" Mom suggests.

"A bath sounds nice," I say.

"Go on, then. Relax."

I stand and make my way upstairs, but I bypass the bathroom and collapse on the twin bed. For a moment, I consider packing a bag and checking into a motel room for the night, so I can sulk in privacy because I know as soon as Weston leaves, my mother is going to have twenty questions for me. Then, I remember there are no rooms available.

I miss my house.

There is no way I'm going to give in and let Damon keep it. He doesn't even like it. Not the same way I do. Every inch of it was built to my specification and decorated by my hand. He just wants to make me angry because he knows he doesn't have any control anymore.

Chapter
twenty-five

Taeli

THE NEXT MORNING, I TELL SARA-BETH AND ERIN EVERYTHING over coffee in the break room.

"You know, if you ever need your own space, you can tell me, and Ted and I will go out for the evening. You can soak in my tub and hang out at my house," Erin offers.

"Thanks, but I'm not running you out of your home," I tell her.

"I might have a solution," Sara-Beth says.

Both of us look at her, and she grins.

"Would you like to take a look at the caretaker's cabin? It's unoccupied at the moment," she asks.

"Caretaker's cabin?"

"Yes. Our former manager used to live there before he met his wife. They bought their house after the wedding, and he moved out. It's been empty ever since," she explains.

"What does he do now?" I ask.

"He and his wife opened the organic pet supply store in town. The cabin has been sitting unused. Hilton intended to have Graham do an addition and update the place to add it to the available vacation rentals, but they haven't gotten around to it yet," she explains.

"Is it close by?" I ask.

"Yes. It's about a half-mile from here. It's on the river. And if you're interested, we can let you use it as part of your salary. All you'd have to do is have utilities hooked up."

"You don't have to do that. Especially if Mr. Tuttle wants to use it for rental income."

She waves me off. "He was married and moved out eight years ago. I don't think Hilton is in any hurry. Besides, it'll be good for you and Caleb to have your own place. Come on. Let's go have a look."

She grabs a set of keys from one of the desk drawers, picks up her purse, and walks to the door, and Erin and I follow. She turns the sign in the window to show that we'll be back in thirty minutes, and the three of us climb into her car.

Ten minutes later, we pull up in front of a tiny post-and-beam cabin in the woods.

"Here we are. What do you think?" she asks as she turns off the ignition.

"It's definitely conveniently located close to the office," Erin encourages.

"Come on. Let's take a look inside," Sara-Beth encourages.

We exit the car and follow her up the three steps to the porch. It's wide, and it stretches across the front and wraps around to a side door close to the parking space.

She takes a key from the pocket of her blazer, inserts it into the lock, and turns. The latch releases, and she pulls open the heavy green door. We walk inside, and she flips a switch on the wall before light fills the space.

Everything is made of wood. The walls. The ceiling. The floor.

That's a lot of wood. Like, a whole lot of wood.

How many trees had to die for this?

"It's small but charming. You just have to use your imagination," Sara-Beth explains.

She walks over to a piece of furniture that is covered with a drop cloth. She takes a corner of the fabric and pulls. A cloud of dust surrounds us as she reveals a soft, well-worn brown leather couch.

"It comes fully furnished. I can't say the furniture is nice, but it's sturdy, and it will get you by until you have the chance to get your own. It has a bedroom and a bath down that hall. The washer and dryer are behind the accordion door. There is a second room and a half-bath off the kitchen. It was used as an office, but it's a good size, and it would make a great room for Caleb."

The kitchen and living room are open with an island separating them, and it has a rock fireplace. She's right. It's charming, and I can see the potential. Besides, it has to be better than sleeping on the twin bed in Mom's sewing room.

"What do you think?" she asks.

I turn to her and smile. "I think it's wonderful."

"I can have the boys come down and get everything uncovered and swept up. It could be ready for you to move in by the end of next week. How does that sound?"

"It sounds like a lot of trouble for you to go through just for us to have a place to stay for another month."

She waves me off. "It's no trouble. We rent places by the day and week. What's a month?" she assures me.

I take a look around.

"Caleb would love being able to walk outside to the river. He's really taken to fly-fishing," Erin says.

"He would," I agree.

"Then, it's settled," Sara-Beth declares.

"Okay, but only if you let me uncover everything and clean it up myself," I tell her.

It's the least I can do, seeing as they are letting us stay for free.

"It's been closed up for a while, and I want to have housekeeping from Rocky Pass come and give it a good scrub down before you bring your son here. Now, let's go grab some lunch and get back to the office," she says without giving me a chance to argue further.

She moves to walk past me and to the door, and I catch her arm. She stops and turns to me.

"Thank you," I choke out, and she pats my hand that is still clutching her.

"You're welcome, Taeli. We are very happy to have you as part of the Rocky Pass family. Even if it is temporary, but I have a sneaking suspicion you're considering staying a bit longer, aren't you?"

I haven't said it out loud to anyone yet, but the more I think about packing up and leaving Balsam Ridge, Mom, my new job, the girls, and Graham to return to face Damon and my shredded life in Illinois, I get nauseous.

"I thought so," she says, reading my thoughts.

"I don't know what to do, Sara-Beth. It's selfish of me to uproot Caleb because I don't want to be there anymore. That makes me no better than Damon. Putting my own wants ahead of his," I cry.

She embraces me.

"The best thing you can do for your son is to give him a happy mother. You need to sit him down and have a conversation with him. Let him be a part of the decision. You might find that he, too, has taken a liking to Balsam Ridge. He deserves to have a voice in it, and you two can decide together," she advises.

I'm on cloud nine when I pick Caleb up for dinner. I decided I needed to take him on a mother-son date tonight. Mom got him ready, and when I pull into the drive, he comes out of the house, clutching a handful of wildflowers he proudly presents to me.

I let him pick where we go to eat, and not surprisingly, he chooses the pizzeria.

We select our slices and take a seat in front of the window that overlooks Main Street. People are milling around on foot, walking to dinner or enjoying a friendly game of miniature golf at the Fantasy Golf and Arcade Room across the street.

"Can we play after we eat?" Caleb asks around a mouthful of pizza.

"Sure. I think we can squeeze in a game or two."

"Yay!"

"I wanted to talk to you one-on-one, bud."

"Okay. What do you want to talk about?" he asks.

"You know how much I like my job, working for Hilton and Sara-Beth, and they really like having the help. So much so that, today, Sara-Beth offered you and me a cabin of our own to stay in. It's a few minutes from the office, the river is in the backyard, and you can walk downtown from it. What do you think?"

He blinks up at me and wrinkles his forehead as he absorbs the information.

"Why do we need a house? You said we were only staying for the summer," he asks.

"I know I did, and I didn't mean to lie to you. I honestly had no idea what would happen once we got here. I just knew we had to leave for me to figure things out."

"So, now, we're just going to live here all the time?" he asks.

"Not if you don't want to."

"But you want to, don't you?" he asks.

"I think I do. I like my job and my friends here. I know Granna loves having us close, and she isn't getting any younger," I explain.

"And you really like Graham," he points out.

"There's that too," I agree.

203

"What about Dad?" he asks, and my heart breaks a little more when I see the pain and uncertainty cross my son's face.

"Dad is staying in Illinois."

"So, we aren't ever going to see him again?" he asks.

I move to him and sit beside him. "Of course you'll see him again. He's your father, and he always will be. Once the divorce is final, we'll hammer out a schedule, so you can spend time with him too."

"Divorce? You never said anything about divorce!"

"I'm telling you now. I know you were hoping we would work things out like before, but some things just can't be worked out," I explain.

"Did you even try?"

"It's complicated, but I promise that we didn't make this decision lightly," I explain.

"What about school and my friends?" he asks.

"We'll enroll you in Balsam Ridge Middle School. It's where I went to school when I was your age. You'll make lots of new friends. I can even talk to them about letting you try out for the soccer team even though they already have a roster. I bet Coach Pittman from your other school would write a recommendation," I tell him.

He turns his eyes to me. "I don't want new friends or a new school."

"Then, we'll go back, and I can find a job in Chicago."

"Dad will support us," he insists.

"Buddy, Dad has a new girlfriend, and they are going to have a baby together."

His eyes go round. "What?"

I take a deep breath. It's time to tell my son the whole truth about why we left. He knew his father and I were fighting, and he knew that his dad moved out, but we'd fought before, and everything worked out. I know, in his mind, he thought it might happen again.

"Do you remember Ivy from your dad's office?"

He nods.

"Well, she and your father became close and …"

"And he cheated on you and made a baby with her?" he asks, his little face turning red.

"Something like that," I whisper.

He jumps to his feet. "I don't want him to have a baby with her," he yells.

"I wasn't thrilled either, but it's not something we can stop," I explain.

"Is that why we came here?"

I nod.

"You said Dad did a bad thing and you needed time apart. I thought he yelled at you or stayed out late or something."

"It was a bit more serious than I let on," I admit.

"Why didn't you say so?"

"Because I didn't want you to worry about this. It's a lot and—"

"I'm not a baby, Mom," he insists.

"No, you're not. I'm sorry I didn't talk to you about everything, but, Caleb, you'll always be my baby, and it's my job to protect you."

Tears threaten to stream down his face, and I can see him trying to hold them back and be strong.

I pat his seat. "Please sit down," I beckon.

He sits back in front of his plate but pushes it aside.

"I don't expect you to understand. I had to get away from there. From everyone and everything because I was never going to heal there. Every person I ran into and every place I entered just threw it in my face. I wasn't enough. And Ivy bouncing around with her baby bump and happy glow was killing me," I confess.

"You should have told me."

"I know. But you're twelve, and it's not your job to worry about my happiness."

"Yes, it is. You're my mom. Don't you worry about my happiness?" he asks.

"Of course I do. Every day."

"Well, the same goes for me. I care if you're sad," he says.

And now, I feel like an ass.

I ruffle his hair. "You know, I forget how grown up you are sometimes. I promise to work on that."

"Can we get my stuff from my old room, or do I have to take Uncle Gene's funiture?" he asks.

"I think we can arrange to have your own things sent down."

He nods.

"You want to give this a shot with me?" I ask.

He taps his fingers on the table like he's thinking hard.

"I guess so," he decides.

"You want to go take a look at it?" I ask, excited to show him the place.

He reaches forward, grabs his second slice of pizza, and takes a bite.

"After I beat you at mini-golf," he says around his mouthful.

"Deal."

Chapter
twenty-six

Graham

MOM AND I HAVE RECRUITED MY BROTHERS TO GET ONE OF our cabins ready for Taeli and Caleb. It was a surprise when she called and announced that they would be moving into the old place. I had no idea she was considering leaving Leona's home.

When I voiced that surprise, Mom shut me down, saying, "She needs more space, and I think it will be good for her and Caleb to have a place to call their own."

When I saw Taeli and Caleb later that day at the Fourth of July picnic celebration, she asked me to take a walk with her and told me about their plans.

"*So, you're staying in Balsam Ridge permanently?*" I asked.

"*We're staying for now. I talked to him and told him everything, and he agreed to give school here a try,*" she said.

I wasn't sure how to react to the news. I hadn't let myself think about the future between us because until now, I hadn't seen a future. She explained that she didn't expect anything from me and that I didn't need to feel obligated to continue whatever was going on between us.

I didn't say a word. Not one damn word. I just walked her back to the crowd, and we ate and went to watch the fireworks, like there wasn't this heavy subject left unresolved.

She was quiet the rest of the evening. Not angry quiet, just unsure.

I hate that I made her feel insecure at all.

I tell Corbin about our conversation.

"What did you say when she told you she was staying?" he asks.

"Nothing."

"Nothing? That's not good," he muses.

"I just needed time to process," I admit.

"And have you?" Corbin asks.

I look over at him as he checks the chimney in the cabin to see if it is safe for use.

"Have I what?"

"Had time to process?"

"Yeah, I have," I admit.

"Well, don't keep us in suspense, bro," Weston calls from the kitchen, where he's hooking up the new dishwasher Mom had delivered.

I look between them. "I'm happy they're staying," I admit.

Weston's eyes go round. "Truly?"

"Yeah, really fucking happy for the first time since I lost my wife. I wake up, looking forward to seeing her face. Neither Leona nor I even make up excuses for me to go by the farm anymore. I just show up because I want to"

Corbin smiles at me. "I called it," he declares.

I raise an eyebrow at him.

"We've been placing bets on whether or not you were falling in love," Morris says as he emerges from the master suite.

"Falling in love?" I ask.

"Yep, Weston and I thought you'd cut and run when it got serious.

Corbin and Langford said you were in it for the long haul, although Langford thought you'd try to deny it for a while longer."

"Nice," I say as I throw the towel I was wiping the walls down with at him.

"Hey, don't take it out on me because you went and lost it over a girl," Morris grumbles.

"At least I have a girl to lose it over," I shoot back at him.

He huffs and tosses it back but misses me.

"I have several women on the hook, I'll have you know," he brags.

"I've seen them, and I'd throw them back if I were you," Weston urges.

"Hey, I have some dope options. You're the one with none."

"By choice," Weston tells him.

"Keep telling yourself that."

They continue the bickering until Pop walks through the front door, lugging a drum sander behind him.

"Fuck, are we resurfacing the floor?" Weston asks.

"Yep," Pop answers.

"Why? It looks fine to me," Morris adds.

"Because your mother said so," Pop tells him.

All three of them groan.

Pop shrugs. "You either do it or go tell her why you think it's unnecessary. I dare you."

Morris walks over and takes the sander from him. "You guys start hauling the furniture out, and I'll start sanding," he grumbles.

"I'll be back with the wood putty and polyurethane," Pop says before disappearing again.

"Your girlfriend is a pain in my ass," Morris says as he passes me to plug in the piece of equipment.

My girlfriend. I like the sound of that.

It takes several hours, but we get the cabin emptied and the floor finished before we pack it in for the night and head out.

Langford and Tucker show up with a couple of sets of bedroom furniture on the back of his truck as I shut the door.

"I've got the stuff Mom wanted out of the storage unit. We need to unload it and put it together," he says.

"No can do. You'll have to take it back along with what's on the trailer hitched to the back of my truck," I inform him.

"Why?"

"Because she made us resurface the floor. We can't move anything back in for at least four days."

He hangs his head. "She rushed me to get this out here. The woman has no concept of how long any of this stuff takes," he complains.

"I know, but in all fairness, she has been trying to get us out here to do some of these things for years now."

"Yeah, I know."

"I'll buy dinner," I tell him.

"All right. Follow me, and we'll take it all to my house and put it in the garage," he suggests.

Langford lives just downriver, and it's a lot closer than the storage unit or my house.

I do as he said.

He pulls his side-by-side out of the second bay of his garage and drives it under his back deck. Then, we carefully stack all the furniture in the space.

"Corbin called and said I owed him fifty bucks. You could have held out a little longer for me," he says.

I shake my head. "I can't believe you assholes were wagering on my love life."

"We bet on everything. You know that," he defends as he shuts the tailgate to his truck and closes the garage door. "I'm glad she's sticking around. She's good for you," he says.

"I don't know what will come of it, but I'm excited to get the chance to find out."

"That's a start," he says. "Now, about dinner. Why don't we order pizza delivery and open a couple of beers? I'll fill you in on Corbin and Susanna's latest drama."

"Lead the way," I tell him.

Chapter
twenty-seven

Taeli

ERIN, JENA, AND ANSLEY SHOW UP TO CELEBRATE US MOVING IN. The place looks so different than it did the day Sara-Beth showed it to me. The old appliances have been replaced with new stainless steel options. The floor has been stained a dark brown, which looks beautiful against the lighter wood of the walls and matches the ceiling beams.

Even though I promised Caleb to have his father send his bedroom furniture from home, Sara-Beth had a great set sent over for each of us until we can have it shipped.

"This place is the cutest," Ansley says as she unloads the bags of groceries they brought for us.

"Isn't it? I never imagined it'd look so good once it was cleaned up," I admit.

"You can hear the river when you sit on the front porch," Erin adds.

"I know. I'll probably spend many evenings curled up out there with a book."

"I don't like to read, but I'd get a swing and listen to it while I napped," Jena says.

They gift me new towels and a faux white fur rug for the living room.

"Thank you, guys, although I have a twelve-year-old boy living with me, so I'm not sure the white rug will last," I tell them.

"We didn't consider that. They had it in off-white and chestnut too. You can exchange it," Erin suggests. "Where is Caleb?" she asks.

"He and Mom had an errand to run. They'll be here later."

Ansley pops the top off a bottle of champagne and pours four glasses. She passes them out and then raises hers.

"To new beginnings," she says, and we all repeat the sentiment and clink our glasses together.

We finish the bottle, and they help me unpack my room and make both of our beds. By the time we settle on the couch, it starts to feel like home.

"I talked to Damon last night," I tell them.

"Why?" Erin asks.

"I had to tell him that we weren't coming back to Illinois at the end of the summer and to warn him that I told Caleb everything, including the baby news."

"How did he take it?" Jena asks.

"Not well. He wants to talk. He asked if he could fly out here."

"What the fuck for?" Erin asks.

"I have no idea."

"What did you say?" Ansley asks.

"I told him there wasn't anything to talk about unless it had to do with Caleb and that coming out here would be a waste of his time and money."

"And?"

"He disagreed. He thinks that there's a lot to talk about. He asked me to come home and to see a counselor with him."

"Therapy? Is he for real?" Jena asks.

"The funny part is, I wanted to see a marriage counselor years ago, after his first affair, and he refused. He thinks psychology is a pseudoscience that has no merit, and he doesn't consider counselors to be real doctors."

"What a title snob," Erin mumbles. "Why now? I thought he was in love with the office tramp," she adds.

"So did I."

"Men make no sense."

"How is Leona doing? Is she sad you guys are moving out?" Jena asks.

"I don't think so. I believe we were cramping her style and cutting into her and Mayor Gentry's alone time." I cringe at the thought.

"I bet she's over the moon that you guys are staying in town though."

"She is. She actually cried when we told her," I confirm.

"That's so sweet," Ansley says.

"And how did Graham take the news?" Erin asks.

"He didn't have much to say about it, to be honest, but Damon sure did. He's planning on fighting me for custody of Caleb."

"What?" Jena gasps.

"I don't know what his game is. I left. I didn't put up any kind of fight. I tried to get him to spend time with Caleb this summer, and he's the one who flaked. Now, he's angry because we're staying here when I told him he could visit anytime he wanted and that we would work out a schedule for birthdays and holidays, so he could see Caleb as much as possible. I'm not trying to keep them apart, but I have to do what's best for me and Caleb."

"Is it a money thing? Like he doesn't want to pay you child support?"

I shrug. "If that's what it's about, he's a bigger asshole than I thought," I say.

"Has his side chick given birth yet?" Erin asks.

"I don't think so, but she is due any day now."

"God help that baby. He doesn't need to be bringing another child into this world," she says.

I don't wish that baby any ill will. It's not the baby's fault how his parents behaved while creating him.

"Hopefully, he does a better job this time around."

One can hope this wasn't all for naught.

Caleb comes through the door with a box in his hand and a smile on his face. Mom and Mayor Gentry follow behind him.

When he makes it to me on the sofa, he stops.

"I have a present for you," he says proudly as he holds the box out for me to take.

"A present? It's not even my birthday," I tell him.

"I know. It's a *just because I love you* present," he says.

My eyes begin to blur before I even get the top off of the little box.

Impatient, he helps me lift the delicate chain and holds the necklace up in front of me.

"Oh, that's beautiful," Ansley says.

He grins at her. "It's a topaz. I found it, and Granna and I took it to a jeweler. He cut it and polished it and made it into a pretty necklace."

"I love it, Caleb," I say through my tears.

"Do you want me to help you put it on?" he asks.

I nod and turn while holding my hair out of the way. It takes him a few tries to get the clasp in place, but when he does, it falls against my chest, and I place my hand over the stone.

"Thank you," I whisper.

He throws his arms around my neck and squeezes. "You're welcome. Next time, I'm going to try to find a ruby or emerald for you."

Jena leans into him. "Hey, your auntie Jena could use an emerald too," she tells him.

"I'll try to get two," he tells her.

"Hey, what about us?" Erin says, waving a finger between herself and Ansley.

Caleb throws his hands out to the sides. "Okay. I'll try to get four. You guys are killing me."

Mayor Gentry starts laughing. "Get used to it, kid," he warns.

"Do you have your bag?" I ask Caleb.

"It's in the car. I'll go get it."

He runs off, and Mayor Gentry follows him.

"The place looks amazing," Mom says as she walks in and pops her head in every door. "Are you excited for your first night?" she asks.

"I am," I admit.

Caleb comes in, carrying his suitcase, and lugs it straight into his new room.

Mayor Gentry appears at the door again.

Mom walks over and kisses my cheek. "We'll get out of your hair. We're going to listen to the bluegrass band down at Blue Mountain Distillery. I'll call you tomorrow."

"Be careful and don't get too crazy," I tell her as I kiss her back.

"No one's getting crazy. We're too old for that," she states.

"Oh, Mom. You're only old when it's convenient for you. Go have fun."

She takes Ralph's arm, and he leads them out.

"I can't believe Leona has a beau, and I'm still single," Ansley mumbles.

"Graham has a couple of single brothers. Maybe Taeli can fix you up," Erin suggests.

"No way. I know Weston too well, and Morris is too young for me."

"What about Corbin?" Jena asks.

"Who would want to deal with Susanna?"

She makes a valid point.

"All I'm saying is, marrying into the Tuttle family would be the answer to all of our middle school dreams," Erin says.

"I outgrew those fantasies a long time ago. I want something real," Ansley tells her.

"Then, we'll find it for you now that we got Taeli here squared away," Erin says.

"I am?"

"Yep. You might not be ready to acknowledge it yet, but you are."

"Well he is taking me out for our second official date tomorrow," I tell them.

"See, you're a taken woman. Taken by a Tuttle," she says, and we all crack up laughing.

But I think she may be right.

The next day Graham picks me up to take me to the winery my mom suggested. It's the perfect place to celebrate my decision to stay in Balsam Ridge.

We enter the gates and drive along the gravel road between vines heavy with plump purple grapes.

A rustic building with a large deck is set in the middle of the vineyard. The deck is dotted with wine barrel tabletops and rich leather stools.

We pull into the parking area, filled with vehicles, to the left of the structure. Employees wearing Shining Rock Winery shirts are milling around on ATVs or sitting atop tractors mowing the grounds between the vines.

There is a small pond in the back of the winery with an old canoe resting on its bank. A couple of elderly gentlemen are sitting on a fallen log beside it with their fishing poles in hand.

"This place is gorgeous," I say, as we exit the truck and walk to the building. The breeze carries a fruity aroma to my nose and I breathe deeply.

"Isn't it?"

He leads me up the steps and to the double glass doors. He opens one side and I step into the large room.

There is a bar to the right with two young ladies attending to a group of women who are tasting the different varieties.

The space has a dozen oak tables with folding chairs. All with a bright floral centerpiece. A stone fireplace is against the back wall with doors on each side that lead to a sunroom that also has tables that line the windows.

A portly man with a round stomach and salt and pepper hair emerges from a side office and greets us.

"Hi, Graham. Who's your friend?"

"Larry, this is Taeli, she's Leona Tilson's daughter."

He grins and extends his hand.

"Well, look at you. I haven't seen you since you were knee-high to a grasshopper."

I place my hand in his and smile.

"You don't remember me, do you?" he asks.

"I'm sorry. I don't," I admit.

"I used to own a cabinetry business in town. I installed the ones in your parent's house when it was built. We also attend the same church," he explains.

"Oh, yes, I remember you. Your wife plays the piano. She gave me lessons when I was little."

"Yes, ma'am that's us. I'm a little long in the tooth now, though. I'm really sorry about your dad. He was a good man and we miss him terribly," he says.

"Thank you."

He releases my hand and looks at Graham.

"Come on in. Have a look around. Once these ladies are finished, we'll set you two up with a wine tasting. The cafe will be opening in about thirty minutes and you can enjoy lunch out on the deck," he invites.

"I was hoping you or your Dad were available to give us a tour," Graham interjects.

"Dad's at home today. Mom had hip replacement surgery and he's playing nursemaid, but I'll be happy to. Just give me five," Larry says, before disappearing back into the office.

When he returns, he takes us down a flight of stairs into the basement. There he shows us the darkroom where the grapes are sorted into white and red. He explains that white grapes are pressed and the juice is immediately sealed into large barrels, yeast is added and the fermentation process begins. However, red grapes are sorted and stored in cold soak tanks to extract the color and flavor from the skin of the fruit before they are pressed and fermented. It's all fascinating. He explains how much sugar is added to qualify the wine as dry, semi-dry, semi-sweet, and sweet. All of their wines are aged in oak barrels to absorb the natural tannins of the wood and the grape to create a perfectly balanced wine, and after eighteen to twenty-four months of storage, they are bottled. We see a bottling demonstration before he leads us outside to the vines.

We walk the property as he gives us the rundown of the planting and harvesting procedures.

"How do you find the time to do this and cabinetry?" I ask, as I pluck a grape and pop it into my mouth. I moan as the sweet juice burst on my tongue.

"I retired from my other job a few years ago. My father suffered a heart attack, and as he was recovering I started researching ways to help him get stronger. Wine, especially the red varieties, is high in resveratrol. Which is a natural antioxidant and helps prevent and manage cardiovascular disease and protects blood vessels from damage. Dad started having three ounces every night while recovering from his by-pass surgery. He started walking and gets stronger every day and now the man can run circles around me. He swears it's the results of the wine."

"He thinks wine saved his life?" I ask.

"He thinks it helped him recover and I believe it did too. Along with many other things. So, I decided it was time to throw caution to the wind and invest in the winemaking business. It was small at first, but we have been adding on every year. First, it was the tasting room, then the deck and now we are a full-time event venue as well. We host everything from festivals, to holiday parties, to several weddings a year out here."

"Wow. Congratulations."

"Thank you. We are certainly blessed."

After the tour, he leads us back inside and sets us up with a tasting. The wines are exquisite. I mark my favorites on the card provided and buy a case to take home.

Graham purchases a bottle of the Pinot Noir and we order salads for lunch.

We settle at a table outside and he pours us each a glass while we wait for our food.

"This was fun. Thank you for bringing me out here," I say.

"It was my pleasure."

"I never thought I'd see the day Balsam Ridge had its own winery."

"We have a distillery, too. We're becoming all kinds of civilized around these parts."

I laugh.

"This would be a beautiful place for a wedding," I muse.

"Yeah, I remember when Heather and I were looking for a venue. There wasn't a lot to choose from back then. We settled for a church ceremony and a reception at my folk's place."

"How long were you two married?" I ask.

"Not long enough," he answers.

Why did I ask that?

"I'm sorry, I don't mean to pry," I apologize.

"It's okay. It was hard for me to talk about at first, but I'm at peace with it now. We were married six years. She was diagnosed with metastatic triple-negative breast cancer a week after our fourth wedding anniversary."

"That must have been a shock."

"It was. She had been feeling poorly for a while. We just thought she had a low immune system. She was always tired, feverish, and became winded easily. She brushed it off as allergies. I mean she was a healthy twenty-five-year-old woman. We never considered it could anything more serious. Until one day I came up behind her while she was at the stove cooking. I picked her up to twirl her around and kiss her when I felt a lump on the side of her right breast close to her armpit. It hadn't been there before. She called the next day and made an appointment with the doctor. It was stage four and had already spread to her liver and lungs."

"Oh my goodness. That's awful. What did they do?" I ask.

"There wasn't much they could do. They talked about a mastectomy, but even with that and chemotherapy, they only gave her a year maybe a year and a half to live. She decided not to endure the surgery. It would be too painful, and the recovery would eat into the time she had left. I fought her on that. I was praying for a miracle and I wanted to do every single thing possible to fight. I was worried more about the length of her days, but she was focused on the quality of the days she had left."

"So, she didn't get any treatment?" I ask.

"She agreed to the chemotherapy. For me. She took three rounds and each time she got weaker and sicker. When they did a scan and saw that it had spread to lesions on her brain and to her bones, despite the aggressive chemo, we stopped the treatment."

"That must have been hard."

"It was. I felt like we were giving up, but my mom sat me down and told me that I could ask her to keep taking the chemo and it may or not extend her life a few weeks, but those weeks would be spent with her too sick to enjoy any time with the people she loved. Or I could spend what time she had left, loving her, laughing with her and making more memories. Memories of peace, instead of sickness. So we stopped everything and brought her home to palliative care. They kept her pain-free and comfortable until the end. She lived another three months."

I feel a tear roll down my cheek. I can see the love in his eyes and the pain in his heart as he talks of her.

"I'm so sorry," I murmur.

His eyes meet mine and he smiles.

"I'm not. I was a lucky man to be the one she loved."

She was the lucky one. How blessed it is to have been loved like that.

"Do you miss her?" I ask.

"Always will, but I don't spend my time thinking about what could have been. I appreciate the time I had with Heather, I treasure our memories, but I don't live in the past. Not anymore."

A server arrives with our lunch, breaking the tense moment. She refills our wine glasses before she walks back inside.

Picking up my glass, I swirl the dark liquid and bring it to my nose. I inhale the aroma before bringing it to my lips and taking a sip.

Graham watches me as I savor the wine.

"Good?"

I lick my lips.

"So good."

We dig in and mom was right, the fig and pear salad is to die for.

"They have concerts out here on the weekends. We should come back," he suggests.

"I'd like that. Thank you for bringing me here today and telling me about Heather."

"I'm happy to tell you anything about my life, Taeli. All you have to do is ask," he says.

And I believe him.

Chapter
twenty-eight

Taeli

I⸺T'S TAKEN US A FEW DAYS TO GET SETTLED IN, AND CALEB AND I ARE anxious to get started on the yard. We woke up early, I make us breakfast, and we discuss our game plan. I am going to tackle the front flower beds and the porch while he uses the weed eater to trim around the house and the outbuilding.

Once I've loaded the dishwasher, we roll our sleeves up and get to work.

By midafternoon, I've already pressure-washed the sidewalk that leads from the parking spaces to the front door, gotten all the cobwebs down, secured the new porch swing, hung three large ferns, which provide some extra sun cover, and transferred the potting soil I purchased to the clay pots on the steps.

My phone rings as I start to weed the flower beds near the mailbox, and I stop to answer.

"Hello."

"Is this Taeli Lowder?"

"Yes, it is."

"This is Shane down at the Jackrabbit Rock Yard. Mrs. Tuttle said you needed some gravel."

"Oh, yes. I want to fill in the driveway at my home. Most of the existing rocks have washed away."

"How much do you want?"

"The driveway is about twenty-five feet by thirty feet," I say, guessing.

"It'll probably take a small truckload," he suggests.

"Okay. I need a truckload delivered, please."

"All right. That'll be two hundred," he says.

"Two hundred dollars? That's all? I said a truckload."

"I heard you," he confirms.

"And the delivery fee. I live off Connelly."

"I know. Sara-Beth told me where you are. That'll be two hundred dollars," he reiterates.

"That can't be right. A five-pound bag is ten dollars apiece at the hardware store," I argue.

"I can charge you more if you insist, but the price is two hundred dollars, delivered, for a small truckload of crush and run."

"All right, if you're sure, I'd like to place an order."

I give him my credit card information and schedule the delivery for Monday. For an extra fifty dollars, they will spread the gravel for me as well.

I finish weeding the beds and plant the flowers I purchased at the nursery in town in the garden and the clay pots. I stand back and examine the work. The pop of color really brightens up the yard.

Caleb comes around the corner with the weed eater in hand.

"I finished the edges," he says.

"Good job, bud."

He joins me, and we both stare at the progress.

"New gravel, a couple of rockers, and a few potted plants on the back deck are all it needs. What do you think?" I ask.

"I like it!"

"Me too," I tell him.

No, it's not the perfectly manicured lawn in the suburbs, but it sure feels more welcoming and cozier than that yard ever did.

It's hard to believe we went from four thousand square feet to just under fifteen hundred square feet, but this tiny cabin in the woods is homier than that pristine palace in the city ever was.

"Can I go wade in the creek?"

I smile down at him. "Sure, just be careful and stay where I can see you out the window."

He runs off behind the house, and I still can't believe my Caleb is running around, barefoot, asking to play in a creek instead of sitting in front of a television.

It's funny how much life can change when you let go of all the wasted space and frivolous stuff. The nonsense you gather and collect that you think makes you look more successful, but in actuality only makes you feel more alone. Daddy used to say a home should be just big enough for you to trip over love every few steps. I didn't understand what he meant back then, but I get it now.

Tucker invites Caleb to a bring-a-friend event with his Boy Scout troop. They are hiking to one of the local waterfalls and then camping in the state park for the night.

Caleb is excited to try Scouts, and I promise that if he enjoys himself, I'll sign him up.

I help him pack his backpack with everything on the list Tucker provided, and Langford picks him up just after three.

I spend the rest of the afternoon hanging blinds and curtains. Then, I light some candles and run me a bath in my new tub to wash away the dirt from my aching body.

I soak for over an hour. It's glorious.

Then, I wrap myself in a fluffy robe, make myself a cup of hot cocoa, and sit out on my porch to watch the sun set.

A star shoots across the clear night sky, and I close my eyes.

"Hope you made a good wish."

I open my eyes at the sound of Graham's sexy, deep voice.

"I'll never tell."

He walks up the steps and joins me on the swing.

I lean into his side, and he wraps an arm around me and tucks me in close.

"This place looks great," he says.

"Yeah, thanks to you and your parents."

"Nah, we made it livable, but you've made it a home," he declares.

"It feels like home," I admit.

"I'm glad," he says before kissing the top of my head.

I look up at him. "You are?"

He slides a finger under my chin and lifts my face to his. "I'm so damn happy you're staying. I'm sorry if I didn't make that clear before," he whispers across my lips before taking my mouth with his.

For the first time in months, I feel free. Free from who I was and what I left behind. Free of the guilt, the embarrassment, and the fear of what is to come. I know that no matter what happens next, I can handle it and that I have people in my life who have my back. It's the best feeling in the world because when you finally decide to let go of all that shit that doesn't matter, you find that you have a free hand to grab the shit that does, so I fist my hands in Graham's shirt and pull him back down for another kiss.

He stops and pulls back. "Caleb?" he asks.

"He's with Tucker's Scout troop," I tell him.

"For how long?"

"They're camping in the state park," I inform him.

"So, we have the cabin to ourselves?"

"Looks like it."

He smiles. "In that case, I have a housewarming gift for you," he says.

"Oh, really?"

He places a kiss on my neck. "Yep. All you have to do is unwrap it," he whispers in my ear.

I stand and extend my hand to him. He takes it, and I lead him inside.

Chapter
twenty-nine

Graham

ONCE INSIDE, SHE LOCKS HER MOUTH WITH MINE, AND I KICK the door shut behind us. I pick her up into my arms and walk her to the master bedroom without disengaging.

She is frantic, and so am I. I set her on her feet at the foot of the bed as I tug at the tie that is holding her robe closed.

She stands before me in nothing but her smile and a pair of red lace panties.

I stalk her until we're near the bed. She squeals as she climbs up and rests against the pillows as I turn and sit on the edge to remove my boots. Impatient, she bears up and wraps her arms around me, tugging at the hem of my shirt. I hold up my arms and let her remove it. She kisses my shoulder and my back as she runs her nails down my chest. I chuckle when she finds the button of my jeans and starts to fumble with it.

I grasp her hand and hold it.

"It's not a race," I tell her, and she laughs.

"I know."

I stand and remove my jeans before climbing back over to her.

I bring my mouth to hers and kiss her softly and slowly. She wraps her legs around my hips to hold me in place.

"Baby, I'm not going anywhere. You don't have to trap me," I whisper against her lips.

She doesn't let me up. She just arches her back and flexes her hips. I groan as the lace grazes my cock. She looks up at me with a glint in her eyes and licks her lips.

"Maybe I like having you trapped," she utters.

"Is that right?" I slide my hand under her ass and lift her as I flip over to my back, bringing her on top.

She grins wickedly as she settles her weight on her knees.

I surrender to her. She can do whatever she likes to me.

She glides her hands over my chest and down my rib cage to the tattoo of my wedding anniversary. Instead of questioning me about it, she simply leans down and brings her lips to my skin.

I take her hair and weave it into my hand, so I can lift it and see her face. Her beautiful face.

I caress her neck right below her ear, and I come up to a sitting position, so I can bring my mouth to the sensitive place where her neck meets her shoulder.

I feel her shudder atop me, and I slowly trail my tongue up the slope of her neck.

She releases a sharp intake of breath as her head falls back, giving me full access to her throat.

God, she is exquisite.

I take my time, savoring the taste of her skin. Absorbing every gasp and moan as I make love to her.

She arches her back and pushes her chest into me, and I feel her seeking my hardness with her core as she begins to move her hips against me.

My cock grows painfully hard at the contact, and I fight the urge to flip her on her back and sink myself deep inside of her.

I want her to take what she wants at the pace she wants it.

I lean back and watch as her breath grows ragged and her eyes roll back as she rides my hips. I grow thicker beneath her. I bring my mouth to her breast, take a taut nipple between my lips, give it a tiny nip, and suck it gently.

She brings her hand to my left bicep and digs her fingernails in sharply as a tremor runs the length of her body.

"Graham," she moans my name, and it breaks the thread of restraint I was holding on to.

I flip her to her back, and her eyes fly open.

"I want to taste you."

I pepper kisses across her stomach and over the top of her panties. She cries out and lifts her hips from the bed, so I can slide them down her legs. I growl as I see how slick and ready she is for me.

I hold her hip with one hand and bring my other to her center, where I dip a finger into her wetness. Her legs start to tremble with anticipation as I circle her clit with my thumb.

She is lying there, naked, completely open to me, and I have never seen anything so fucking beautiful in my life.

I slide my hands under her and bring my mouth to her core. I lick and suck and savor her. She threads her fingers into my hair and pulls as I bury my tongue inside of her and let her ride it. Then, I add a finger and then another till she is completely full. Her hips begin jerking uncontrollably, and she starts holding her breath as her orgasm hits her.

I lap every last drop from her before I crawl up her body and take her mouth in a possessive kiss.

She drops her knees, spreading for me, and takes my throbbing cock into her hand. She strokes me a couple of times before she brings me to her entrance, and I thrust into her. She is so hot and ready and perfect. I try to go slow and easy, but I'm too far gone. I pump into her rhythmically as she scores my back with her nails. She raises her hips to meet each thrust to bring me deeper inside.

I pull back, trying to get control of myself because I'm about to come and I want it to last longer, but she tightens her muscles around me.

Fuck me, that feels amazing.

I give in, and I move harder and faster until I explode. My release rockets down my spine and into her. She wraps her arms around my neck and holds me tight as she comes hard again.

I stretch out, covering her, as our breathing evens out. We are a sweaty, sated mess, tangled in her new bedsheets.

When my heart rate finally calms down, I look into her beautiful amber eyes, and for the first time in years, I feel like I'm home.

I get up and run to the bathroom. I come back with a warm towel to find her fast asleep. I take a pillow and gently lift her head and place it under her. Then, I lie beside her and tuck her into my side.

I hold her all night. Every thread of apprehension inside my chest snaps loose.

I'm in love with this woman.

Chapter
thirty

Taeli

I AWAKEN IN GRAHAM'S ARMS. I ROLL OVER AND SNUGGLE INTO HIM and close my eyes. Never have I felt so enveloped in strength and comfort. I tangle a finger into the hair on his chest and tug lightly. He flinches in his sleep and covers my hand with his. I try to pull my hand loose, and his grip tightens.

"What are you doing?"

His gravelly voice makes me open my eyes again and smile against his side.

"Nothing." I feign innocence.

One of his eyes pops open and looks down at me.

"Vixen," he accuses.

I roll up onto an elbow and begin to pepper kisses up his side and around to his chest. I nip at one of his nipples, and he swats at me, which urges me forward.

I glide one hand under the covers and find his hard shaft waiting for my attention.

I wrap my fingers around his velvety flesh and get a firm hold.

He groans as he pushes the sheets away from his hips, so he can watch as I begin to slowly pump my fist up and down as he grows harder in my grip.

His hand that my head is cradled on top, moves to rub circles on my rib cage and then comes under my arm to squeeze one of my breasts.

I slide my left leg over the top of his and bring my core to his side. I begin to glide against him as I continue to pull and rotate his sensitive flesh.

He watches me intently as his breath quickens.

My hips start to move faster against him, seeking the friction I need. I watch in fascination as the muscles of his abdomen contract with each pump of my fist. Just when I think he is about to explode, I release him, and a soft curse escapes his lips.

I slide my leg on over his lap, and he groans as my wetness catches the tip of his cock.

I pull up, and he reaches for my hips to bring me back down on him, but I slide downward before he can stop me. I kiss the inside of his thigh, and it twitches. Then, I take him back in my hand and hold him up, so I can find his balls with my tongue.

His hips jump up off the bed, and I wait until he settles back down to run my tongue up his length. I lick the salty bead that has escaped. Then, I suck his tip into my mouth, swirling my tongue as I do.

"Fuck," he mutters as he gathers my hair away from my face so he can see me.

I begin to suck him deeper until he hits the back of my throat.

"There's nothing sexier than watching you take me in your mouth," he says, his eyes boring into mine as I take him deeply again and again.

I listen as his breaths come faster, and that's when I rake my teeth across his tip.

"I'm going to come, baby," he warns.

Instead of backing off, I suck harder, and he explodes. His warm release hits the back of my throat.

His head is thrown back against the pillow, and his eyes are shut as I swallow every drop until he is completely spent.

Then, I crawl up his body and wrap myself around him, and he holds me, skin to skin.

"Now, that's a good morning," he mumbles, and I snuggle in closer and drift back off to sleep.

We awaken to a knock at the door.

I jump up to look at the clock on the nightstand, and it's almost noon.

I grab my robe from the floor beside the bed and pull it on.

"You expecting company?" Graham asks as he watches me frantically trying to locate my underwear.

"No. You?" I ask.

"Nobody even knows I'm here," he tells me.

"Your truck is in the driveway."

"Oh yeah," he says.

"You stay here, and I'll get rid of whoever it is," I instruct, and he gives me a salute.

I roll my eyes and sprint to the front door.

I peer out the peephole and see my son's face staring back at me. *Shit.*

Panic wells up in my chest as his impatient knuckles pound on the wood again.

I run back into the bedroom to find Graham pulling on his jeans.

"It's Caleb. Oh my God, oh my God," I whisper-yell.

His eyes come up to mine.

The bastard grins.

"Graham, what do I do?" I ask.

"Nothing. Just stay here," he says before casually strolling out of the room, shutting the door behind him.

I place my ear against it and strain to listen.

Graham opens the door, and I hear Caleb ask him what he's doing here.

"Sara-Beth sent me over to look at the new dishwasher. She said your mom called last night because it was making a racket," Graham replies.

"Where's Mom?" Caleb asks.

"She said she was going to take a shower while I fixed this thing, so she would be ready when it was time to pick you up. I guess she's still in there."

"One of the boys got stung by a bee during breakfast, and his face swelled up like a balloon. It was gnarly. The troop leader had to take him to the emergency room, so he called everyone's parents to pick us up early. Tucker's dad dropped me off."

"A bee sting, huh? That sucks."

"Yeah, he's allergic. He had his EpiPen in his backpack, but his face was messed up."

"Speaking of breakfast, maybe you and I should make some for your mom. She's going to be surprised when she walks out and you're already home."

"What about the dishwasher?" Caleb asks him.

"Already done. It was a loose bolt. I should have known better than to let Weston install it."

"Yeah, you should have."

Caleb giggles, and I back away from the door, careful not to make any noise. Then, I slip into the shower and let the spray wash over me quickly.

When I enter the living room about twenty minutes later, I find the two of them at the stove. Caleb is stirring a pan of scrambled eggs, and Graham is browning sausage links.

"What's this?" I say, and they turn to me.

"Good morning, Mom. Graham and I are making breakfast."

I fold my arms over my chest. "I can see that. How did you get here?" I ask.

"It's a long story. I'll tell you over breakfast," he replies.

"Can I help?" I offer.

"Nope. Graham and I have it under control. Don't we?" he asks Graham, who looks over his shoulder at me and winks.

"We sure do. You just take a seat at the table, and we'll be right with you."

I do as I was told and take a seat, watching my two favorite guys make my breakfast.

Chapter
thirty-one

Taeli

AFTER BREAKFAST, I WALK TO MY OFFICE WHILE CALEB RIDES with Graham to check on the theme park construction site.

I don't normally work on Sundays, but it's been a busy couple of weeks with everyone wanting to get one last family vacation in before schools start back, so I told Sara-Beth I'd come in for a few hours to help her and Erin with checkouts.

When I round the entrance to the campground, I see a truck backed up to the door and a delivery driver hauling roses inside.

I climb the steps and follow him to find the entire office covered in flowers.

Roses of every color.

Dozens and dozens of them.

"What is going on?" I ask.

Sara-Beth's head pops up from behind the vases that are stacked on my desk.

"Taeli, I think you have an admirer," she states.

Me?

She doesn't mean these are for me. When would Graham have ordered them? He wasn't out of my and Caleb's presence this morning.

"Yes, you," Erin says as she comes down the hall.

The driver looks at me. "You must be Mrs. Lowder."

I nod.

"Here's the card," he says, handing me an envelope.

"Wait, you aren't leaving all of these here, are you?" I ask as he turns to exit.

"Yep. They're all yours."

I turn back to the room and the insane display.

"Are you going to open that?" Erin asks.

I look at the envelope in my hand and slide my fingers under the lip.

I tug a slip of paper from inside with a handwritten note. I recognize the handwriting immediately.

Damon.

"What does it say?" Sara-Beth asks as they both come to join me.

"It's from my husband."

"Are you serious?" Erin cries.

I hand the card to her, and she reads his words aloud. *"Taeli, I'm so sorry. I was stupid. Please forgive me. I love you. Damon."* She looks up at me.

"That man has some nerve," Sara-Beth says.

"And deep pockets. These things had to have cost a fortune. What are you going to do with all of them?" Erin asks.

"Take them to all the shops and motels in the valley," I suggest.

"I'll call Hilton," Sara-Beth says before hurrying behind the desk and picking up the phone.

Erin moves beside me. "I guess you deciding not to come back really rattled his cage, huh?"

"Yeah, that and a new baby."

I bet Ivy finally went into labor.

"Hilton and Corbin are on the way to take care of them," Sara-Beth informs us.

"Good. Now, let's get some work done," I say.

We do just that while the guys load the unwanted floral display into their trucks and take them to brighten the day of every working lady in the valley.

Once we are all caught up, Erin drives me home, where we find Damon perched on my new porch swing.

I see red.

"Is that who I think it is?" she asks.

"Yep," I answer. I don't even wait until her car comes to a full stop before I open the door and jump out.

Damon stands and meets me at the steps.

"You're insane. You do realize that, don't you?" I scream.

"Calm down, Taeli."

"Don't tell me what to do. You covered my office in thousands of dollars of roses. I don't even like roses."

He gets a perplexed look. "I thought they were your favorite flower," he says.

"No, irises are my favorite flower."

"Why didn't you ever tell me that?"

"I did. We had irises at our wedding. I have an iris tattooed on my hip. And I named the puppy you bought me Iris."

"Oh, I didn't correlate them."

"Of course you didn't."

Erin gets out of her car, slams her door shut, and stands beside it.

"Who's that?" Damon asks as he looks over my shoulder to the driveway.

"One of my best friends," I tell him.

"Don't be silly. Michelle is your best friend. Has been for years."

I bristle at that and dig in my purse for my keys.

"Michelle is not my friend. Neither is Amy nor Mandy for that matter."

"But this person is all of a sudden?"

"That's right," I say as I locate my keys and walk past him to the door.

He reaches out and clasps my arm. "Taeli, wait. I just want to talk, please."

"Do you need me to get the Taser out of my glove compartment?" Erin calls.

I shake my head and then stop and turn back to her. "You have a Taser in your car?"

"Girl, yes. You never know when you're going to run up on a bear."

"She's crazy," Damon mumbles.

My head snaps back to him. "No, she's not, but you definitely are. What are you doing here? Isn't Ivy due any minute now?"

"Probably."

"You left her and came here? Why would you do that?"

He hangs his head. "Because I love you. I want you. I've always wanted you. She was a distraction. A stress reliever. A silly fling that didn't mean anything," he blurts out.

"The fuck?" Erin mutters.

I laugh. "Translation: she is hot, fun, and young, and she was convenient until she ended up pregnant, and now, it's not so fun, right?" I spit.

"Taeli, baby." His voice cracks with emotion.

"Don't do that. Don't think you can show up here and shed tears and make it all better. Just because you want me doesn't mean you value me, I need to be valued, Damon."

"This is about him, isn't it?" he asks.

"Who?"

"Graham Tuttle. Of course you come to Balsam Ridge and link

up with one of the Tuttles. What? Were you in search of a bigger, better deal?" He hurls the accusation.

"Are you serious right now?"

"Dead serious. You're sleeping with him, aren't you?"

"That's none of your business."

"You're my wife!"

"That didn't matter to you when you were screwing your assistant, now did it?"

"Damn. I'm calling Jena and telling her to bring some popcorn," Erin says before pulling her phone from her back pocket.

"You want the truth? You're right. He is part of it. I like him. I like him a hell of a lot. I might even love him."

His eyes fill with rage. "And you think you can trust him? You barely know him."

"I know I can," I insist.

"Yeah, well, you trusted me once too. So, maybe you aren't the best judge of character."

"Did you really just say that, dude?" Erin asks.

He ignores her.

"You don't get to question me. You broke us. You broke me. I don't owe you any apologies for what it took to heal what you crushed. So stop with the guilt. I can move on with whomever I choose," I retort.

"I don't want you to make another mistake. We can fix this," he insists.

"You just called me out for being stupid for trusting you and called yourself a mistake," I say.

"You're twisting my words."

"No, I'm pointing out how ridiculous you sound right now."

"You can't love him," he states matter-of-factly.

"Yes, I can. It's a different kind of love. It's grown-up love, and it fucking rocks."

"Oh, snap," Erin says.

The words hit him like physical blows.

"Taeli," he pleads.

"You don't get it. You ruined us and now it's like the ground split open and we're standing on opposite sides of this great abyss that neither can cross. Go home, Damon. There is no path back to us."

He sniffles as I watch the fight leave him.

"I don't like who I am without you," he utters.

"Too bad because I love who I am without you."

He takes a step back, and then he sits on the top step. He honestly thought I'd run into his arms.

"Go home, Damon, and maybe this time around, you can fix all the mistakes we made. That's what I'm trying to do."

"I made a mistake, okay? A stupid mistake. We can get past this."

I take a seat beside him just as Jena pulls up and Erin hurries to her passenger side and gets in.

"No. A mistake I could forgive. You made a choice. A choice to fuck up our family. And if I'm being honest, I'm glad you did. You released me from the Stepford nightmare I was living in."

"I know I fucked up, but you're the one who left."

"You said you were in love with another woman. What did you expect me to do?" I ask.

"I expected you to stay and fight for us like before, but you just walked out."

"And you let me without so much as shedding a tear. What does that tell you?" I ask.

"I can't believe it's over. I never thought we'd get here. That one day, I'd push you too far that we couldn't find our way back," he admits.

"Really? You thought I'd sweep a new baby under the rug and still show up at the club for lunch, as if nothing happened?" I ask incredulously.

"I never meant for that to happen, I swear."

"It's my fault too. Somewhere along the way, I stopped being me and started being Dr. Lowder's wife. I played in a neighborhood Bunco league, for goodness' sake. I forgot who I was."

"She's still in there. I see her now."

"Yeah, she is."

"What about Caleb? I might have to let you go, but he is my son, and I will not give up on him. I'll fight for my boy."

"God, I hope so. He needs to know you want him, but you can work on your relationship with him later. Now, I think you need to get back to Ivy ASAP."

"Yeah. I can send him some things for his room and maybe a new television for your living room."

"No, you can't buy his love, and you have to stop trying. It just makes things worse. He's not going to remember the number of presents under the tree on Christmas morning. He won't be able to recall how much the shoes on his feet cost or the thread count of his sheets on his bunk bed. He's going to remember the time you spent with him and the memories you put in the effort to make together."

"I think I've already blown it. We don't have a lot of father-son memories."

I shrug. "History is always in the making. You can start now and get it right, going forward. Now, about Ivy," I press.

"She isn't speaking to me, I'm sure."

"Well, pal, you deserve her wrath. Maybe a hospital room full of roses will do the trick. It can't hurt to try."

I stand, and he stands with me.

"I still love you. I hurt the best person I've ever known, and I'm kicking myself for it."

"Good. Just don't do it forever. We both need to move forward."

"Can I wait for Caleb?"

I sigh and point to the swing.

I text Graham and ask him to bring Caleb home. Then, I leave Damon and walk down and climb into the backseat of Jena's car.

"What's the verdict? Is he just going to hang outside your house forever?" Jena asks.

"He's waiting for Graham to bring Caleb home, so he can see him."

"That won't be awkward at all," Jena says.

"Tell me about it."

"Here." She hands me a bag.

"You actually brought popcorn?" I ask.

"Yeah, Erin said come quick and bring popcorn. So I grabbed popcorn and sped over."

"Did she even tell you why?" I ask.

"Dude, she didn't have to. Come quick and bring popcorn is code for some shit is about to go down and she needs someone to watch it with. You don't ask questions at that point, you just get in the car," she explains.

"What if she was in trouble and needed help of some sort?"

"Then she would have said come quick and bring your gun. That's totally different," she clarifies.

"Yep, no time for popcorn in that situation," Erin agrees.

"Got it," I tell them.

"I did bring a shovel though, just in case. It's in the trunk," Jena informs.

"Good thinking. Graham might beat Damon to death and we'll need it," Erin says.

"Graham's not going to fight Damon," I insist.

"You're probably right. We may have to do it ourselves," Erin offers.

"No one is fighting Damon. Caleb is on his way," I remind them.

"Shoot, kids are always ruining our fun," Jena grumbles.

"Speaking of Graham, you love him. You love Graham Tuttle," Erin teases.

"No, I don't," I deny.

"Oh, yes, you do. You two are like two olives in a martini. We just heard you admit it."

I shake my head. "I couldn't possibly. It's only been a couple of months. That's too soon for love," I insist, "but I do feel something that could grow into love."

Jena laughs. "Girl, life doesn't always work out on a neat time-table. The heart doesn't give a shit about time. Our brain calculates time, but our heart just feels, and it doesn't care if it's been a month or if it's been ten years. If it finds something true, it just runs with it. Let yourself run toward happiness. Don't let your brain take the lead this time. Tell it to shut the hell up and go get that man," she advises.

I look up at my front porch. "I think that will have to wait until I can get rid of this man."

"No doubt," she agrees.

Chapter
thirty-two

Graham

After receiving Taeli's text, Mom's call, and Erin's text, I prepare Caleb for what he'll find when we make it to his home.

"I don't understand why he'd come here," Caleb says.

"I don't know, bud, but you'll get a chance to ask him."

He nods and stares straight ahead until we pull up to the cabin.

When he spots his father on the porch, he exits the truck and marches up to him. I stay at his flank in case he needs reinforcement.

"Hey, son," Damon greets.

"Dad," Caleb responds.

"I just wanted to apologize for hurting you. I didn't mean to."

"I'm not mad at you because you hurt me. I'm mad because you hurt Mom. You made her cry. You're supposed to be the one she can count on. The one who makes her feel good and safe," Caleb accuses.

"Son, sometimes, grown-ups—" Damon starts.

"Don't feed me a bunch of bullshit excuses, Dad," Caleb shouts.

"Watch your mouth, young man," Damon scolds.

"No."

"Caleb!" Damon raises his voice, and Caleb flinches.

"Dad." Caleb stands his ground and doesn't so much as blink as he stares his father down.

Damon finally slumps and goes to a knee to look his son in the eye. "Look, I know I messed up. That's why I'm here. I've apologized to your mother, and I owe you an apology too. I'm sorry, son. I had hoped the two of you would come home with me. That's not going to happen, but you can still come home if you want."

Caleb shakes his head. "No. I don't want to go back. I like it here. I like seeing Mom smile and laugh. I like seeing her being treated like she matters. That's the kind of man I want to be. One whose family knows they can count on me to be there for them. To love them. To teach them how to fish and change a flat tire. I want to come home to my family at night and actually be there with them. Eat dinner and talk about things."

"I know I haven't spent a lot of time with you. I work a lot. Too much. But I love you, son. You and your mother."

"I love you too. I always will, but I don't respect you anymore. Granna says that love is something you give your family freely, but respect is something they have to earn. We need both. Me and Mom. We need both." His voice cracks on the last words.

I fight the urge to wrap an arm around him. I turn and see the same thing warring in Taeli as she clutches the seat in Jena's car while watching her son confront his father.

"Granna is a hundred percent correct, and I promise to do better from now on," Damon tells him.

Caleb walks the few steps that are left between them and into his father's open arms.

"How long do we have before you leave?" Caleb asks.

Damon looks down at his watch. "Four hours. Not very long, son," he answers.

Caleb shrugs. "It's more than we had yesterday."

Damon smiles at him. "That's true. Do you want to go grab a burger or something?" he asks.

"Sure. Let me go to the bathroom, and I'll be right back."

He runs inside, and Damon watches as the door closes behind him. Then, he turns back to me, and I smile.

"What's so fucking funny?" he asks.

I shake my head. "You wanting a second chance. Expecting one, like it's your right to have it," I answer.

"You think I don't deserve one?"

"You were lucky to have the first chance, and you wasted it, so no, I don't think you do."

"You don't know anything about me," he snaps.

"I know you like to have your cake and eat it too. You had a fucking prize at home, yet you still needed to mess around with any woman who batted her eyelashes at you. You probably wanted to make your wife jealous. To stroke your ego. But a real man doesn't make his woman jealous of other women. He loves her in a way that makes other women jealous of her."

He leans into my face and repeats himself.

"You don't know me."

"Maybe I don't, but I know men like you, and I think you deserve to have your ass handed to you for the way you treated your family."

"You want to take a swing at me?" he asks.

I shake my head. "Nah, but I bet you want to take one at me."

"I do."

I walk toward him, and he takes a step backward. I extend my hand.

"I don't want to punch you. I want to shake your hand and say thank you for letting her go."

He looks at my hand like it's on fire.

"She's too good for you too," he spits.

"The greatest gift a father can give his children is to love their mother and to treat her with respect. My pop taught me that, not with his words, but by the way he looked at, spoke to, and handled my mother every day of my life. He didn't need to say it. He lived it, but you're gonna have to live with the guilt of what you put your wife and the mother of your child through. I know that she left because she was ashamed, but you're the one who should feel shame for the rest of your days. And I know she's too good for me, but I'm willing to spend the rest of my life trying to be good enough for her."

He looks over my shoulder to where the girls are sitting in the car.

I know they can hear every word.

I don't care.

The front door opens again, and Caleb reappears.

"I'm ready," he calls.

Damon smiles at his son. "So am I."

He calls out to Taeli, "I'll have him back before I head to the airport."

"Okay. Just text me when you're on your way," she yells out the back window.

Caleb looks at me. "Can we check on the theme park tomorrow?" he asks.

"Sure we can. You go have fun with your dad."

He breaks away and runs down to me. He wraps his arms around my waist and squeezes. "Thanks," he says.

I place a hand on his head. "You're welcome."

"That four-hour window is dwindling, Caleb," Damon says.

He releases me, and then he trots back over and takes his father's hand.

Taeli, Erin, and Jena exit the vehicle and stand with me as we watch the two of them drive away.

Erin pats my back. "You handled that well, big boy," she praises.

"Yeah, I would've kneed him in the nuts, for sure. Way to keep your crazy tucked in," Jena adds.

"Uh-oh. Here come the blue-haired gangsters," Erin says as Leona's Jeep comes screeching to a halt in front of us, my mother riding shotgun.

"What are you doing?" Taeli asks when they step out.

"Coming to help," Leona says.

"Help how exactly?" I ask.

She shrugs.

"You're here to watch the carnage," Taeli accuses.

"No, we're not."

People rush to see the wreckage and delight in others' suffering. It might sound cynical, but it's true.

Traffic is brought to a standstill while onlookers gawk at an accident by the side of the road. Bystanders use their phones to video a fire or an arrest. Viewers watch footage of damage caused by floods or hurricanes with bated breath.

Cyberbullies sit behind a computer screen and tear some teenagers down for their amusement. It's all just one big, ugly crowd-pleaser. Like when we'd all go running outside to watch when someone yelled, "Fight," in the school cafeteria.

"Yes, you are. But it's okay. We all do it. Why do you think Jena rushed over with the popcorn? The ancient Romans actually forced people to fight to the death for sport, and the people of Massachusetts cheered at the Salem witch trials. We're all masochists at heart. It's human nature," Erin says.

Leona turns to her. "You scare me sometimes."

Erin just grins.

Chapter
thirty-three

Taeli

MOM AND SARA-BETH STAY LONG AFTER ERIN AND JENA HEAD home.

They raid my refrigerator and throw together a chicken Alfredo for dinner.

I'm too nervous to eat as I wait for Caleb to return home. I hope his time with his father isn't spoiled by our drama. Hopefully, Damon is able to set our adult bullshit aside and focus on his son.

"You're going to pace a hole in the newly refinished floor," Mom says as she hands me a glass of wine.

I take a huge gulp and continue my path to the window and back.

Graham catches me as I turn again, and he wraps his arms around me.

I let him hold me and absorb his strength.

"Thank you for staying with me. I don't think I could have handled Mom alone right now."

He leans back and takes my face in his hands. "Where else would I be?" he asks.

My eyes fill with tears. He dips his head and kisses the corner of my left eye to catch one before it flows down my cheek.

"Calm down. Caleb is going to be fine," he assures me.

I relax against him.

"There, that's better," he says.

"I'm sorry about Damon. I can't believe he said all of that to you."

"I can. He could see it, and it was killing him," he says.

"See what?" I ask.

"How much you and Caleb mean to me and how much I mean to you guys."

I go still.

"How much do we mean to you?" I ask. I regret the words as soon as they leave my lips.

"Everything," he whispers, and I feel the depth of that one word in my soul.

"Graham." His name is a plea on my lips.

He leans in and kisses me. It's a long, deep, and claiming kiss.

A throat clears, and we break apart to see Mom and Sara-Beth at the door.

"We're going to go. You can have Caleb call me to check in when he gets home," Mom tells me.

"I will. Thanks for everything, Mom."

"Oh, I should be thanking you, kiddo."

"For what?"

"Bringing my family home."

She blows me a kiss, and then they are gone, leaving Graham and me alone.

"What do we do now?" I ask.

"I can think of a few things that might distract you," he growls.

"Don't threaten me with a good time, mister," I tease.

He starts walking us toward the bedroom when the front door swings open. Caleb finds me in Graham's arms, and I don't step away.

He looks at us and grins.

"Gross," he says. "You two aren't gonna walk around, kissing each other all the time now, are you?"

"Probably so, kiddo," I admit.

"Try to keep it to a reasonable level, okay?" he requests.

"We can do that." Then, I ask him, "How did things go with your dad?"

He shrugs.

"We ate burgers."

Well, that's a very male answer.

I roll my eyes.

"Anything else to report?" I prompt.

"He wants me to come to Chicago for Labor Day and meet my baby brother."

"And how do you feel about that?" I ask.

"I told him that as long as there are no fireworks or Boy Scouts events that weekend, I'll consider it."

Graham laughs.

Caleb cuts his eyes to him.

"So, are you guys boyfriend and girlfriend now?" he asks.

Graham looks at me and smiles. Then, he clasps my hand, interlocking our fingers. "We are."

"Good. I like you, and if you two end up married, Tucker and I will be cousins, which would be super cool."

I cough.

"No one is talking marriage," I assure him.

"Bummer." He heads for his room.

"I guess that means we have his blessing," I say.

"Whew. He had me sweating there for a minute," Graham states.

"Me too," I agree.

Caleb's door clicks shut, and Graham grins at me.

"Where were we?" he asks.

"We were about to clean the kitchen," I tease.

He rests his forehead against mine.

"I'll need a cold shower first," he mumbles, and I burst into laughter.

I wrap my arm around his neck.

"Looks like you don't have to envy the trees any longer," he whispers against my lips.

"Nope. I'm ready to let go and let the new in."

"We're going to be a great adventure," he promises, and then he kisses me, and then we get to cleaning the kitchen.

epilogue

Taeli
One Year Later

"I HAVE ONE!" I SQUEAL, AS I REEL IN THE GORGEOUS RAINBOW trout.

I've been honing my fly-fishing skills this past year. It's something that both my guys enjoy and has become an unspoken competition among the three of us. Caleb keeps a mental count of catches and weights. Graham is in the lead, but Caleb is right on his heels. I'm determined to overtake my son.

When Graham asked if I wanted to go out today, I jumped at the chance. Caleb's baby brother's first birthday was last weekend and he flew to Illinois to attend the party; therefore, I have a chance to advance in the game while he's gone.

Graham steps forward and takes the fish in his hands and uses a set of pliers to remove the hook. Once it's free from my line he holds it up.

"It's a beauty. I bet this one will come in around twelve pounds," he praises.

"Every ounce helps," I declare.

He takes the trout and adds it to our cooler of ice.

"Do you want to go again?" he asks.

I look up. The sun is beginning to set, and the sky is aglow in a breathtaking array of pink and orange. I will never tire of the beauty of dusk in the Tennessee mountains.

"It's getting late," I muse.

He follows my gaze and agrees.

"Yeah, but I think we can cast one more time before it's dark. You may even be able to slip into second place if your able to pull in another ten-pounder."

Second place? I didn't think I was that close.

"Really? Caleb is going to accuse me of cheating for going out while he's at his dad's."

He shrugs.

"So, what? He'll pass you again next weekend."

That's true. I don't stand a chance.

"Let's do it," I decide.

He smiles and walks over to take my rod.

"You want to try a wet fly this time? Caleb and I tied a few ourselves. Grab one out of my tackle box," he instructs, and I trudge my way out of the water to the blanket holding our gear.

"Which ones are the wet flies?" I ask as I lift the top of the box.

"The second row from the top. There should be a bright yellow one on the right," he calls.

"Got it!"

I gasp when the light from my headlamp catches a glint as I snatch it from the kit.

A large round diamond ring is dangling from the lure.

I turn on trembling legs to find that Graham has made his way to the edge of the creek and is standing behind me. He reaches out and takes my hand to steady me.

"What is this?" I ask.

He sinks to one knee before me and looks up to meet my eyes.

"I never thought that I could find love again. I was perfectly content living the rest of my life alone until you and Caleb came barreling into Balsam Ridge and into my path. I love you, Taeli. I love your son. I know you've been through hell and so have I, but we've both been given a second chance and I'd be the happiest man on earth if you'd agree to be my wife. Say yes, and let's grow our family and build an amazing life together."

I cover my mouth with my free hand and let the beauty of the moment wash over me. This man is on his knee with the sunset at his back, pledging to love me and Caleb for the rest of our lives.

How did I get so lucky?

"Please?" he whispers.

I laugh as I let the tears I've been holding back flow down my cheeks and choke out my answer.

"Yes, yes, yes!"

I fall to my knees in front of him as he unties the ring and slides it on my finger. Then I wrap my arms around his neck and press my lips to his.

Graham

She said yes.

I stand bringing her up with me and twirl her in my arms.

I was so nervous trying to pull this moment off and the weight of that rolls off my shoulders and all I feel is relief and immense joy.

"I have another surprise," I whisper into her neck.

She bears back and looks at me.

"Really?"

The glow of happiness that she is wearing makes my heart skip.

"Yep, let's get packed up and head to the truck."

We gather our things and strip out of our waders.

I drive us to my parent's home sitting on top of the mountain overlooking the valley.

Our friends and family are waiting inside to help us celebrate.

As we exit the truck, Caleb, who was standing on the front porch, comes running to us.

"What are you doing here? I thought you were still in Chicago?" she cries, as he embraces her.

"Nope. We tricked you. I flew home this morning and Granna picked me up at the airport," he tells her, then takes her hand and leads us toward the house.

"Come on. SaraBeth and Granna made us dinner."

He opens the door and as Taeli steps over the threshold, he begins to giggle.

"Surprise!"

Everyone begins to shout and cheer as we enter the kitchen. Langford slaps me on the back and each of my brothers shakes my hand. Leona takes Taeli's face in her hands before hugging her daughter tightly and giving me a wet wink over her shoulder.

The girls grab Taeli and pull her toward the sunroom to admire the ring. I watch as they gush over the jewelry and start snapping photos. Then I walk over to the island and kiss my mother's cheek as she and Pop fret over her phone.

"Thank you for this, Mom."

"You're welcome," she says, as she looks to me. I see the crease on her brow and step closer.

"What's going on?" I ask as my eyes meet Pops.

He turns the phone screen to me.

"Looks like Garrett is heading home," he says.

What kind of trouble has my wayward brother gotten himself into now?

the end

Prologue

Gabby
Four Years Old

I AM GETTING ALL DRESSED UP LIKE A PRINCESS.

Papa and Mamma are expecting company for dinner to-night, so Nonna has dressed me in my prettiest dress. It is pur-ple, and it has yellow butterflies on the front. Purple is my favorite color.

I twirl and twirl until I'm dizzy.

"Hold still, so I can finish your hair, Gabriella," Nonna scolds.

She helps me get my shoes on as she explains that the Scutari family just moved two estates down from us. Mr. Scutari is in the same business as Papa. He and his three boys—Emilio, Atelo, and Christoff—as well as their grandparents are coming to meet us all tonight, and Papa wants me and my brothers to be on our very best behavior. She holds my hand and leads me downstairs.

"There is my *bambina*." Papa reaches out for me, and he picks me up and spins me around as I laugh with glee. He turns, and I see a group of people huddled in the foyer.

"Say hello to our new friends, Gabriella. This is Papa's friend Mr. Scutari and his boys and their grandparents."

"Hi." I wave shyly and lay my head on Papa's shoulder.

They all say hello in return, and Papa shows us into the dining room where Mamma and Nonna are placing food in the center of the table. My tummy growls loudly, and everyone laughs.

"My baby girl is always hungry." Papa smiles down at me as he places me in my seat between Nicco and one of his friend's sons.

I sneak a peek up at the stranger. He has long, dark hair that falls into his face. His eyes are dark green, and when he smiles down at me, he has a dimple in his cheek, just like Nicco.

"Hey, I'm Christoff."

"Where is your mamma, Crisscross?" I ask.

"No, Chris-toff," he repeats.

I wrinkle my nose. That's what I said.

I mimic him, "Criss-cross."

He laughs, and so does Nicco.

"Gabriella, he said Christoff, not Crisscross. Crisscross would be a silly name."

"I didn't say Crisscross. I said, Criss-Cross," I state in aggravation.

"You just said it again."

"I did not."

Nicco is always mean to me, and he always tries to embarrass me.

"It's okay," Christoff whispers to me. "You can call me Crisscross if you want to."

"I don't want to call you that. People will laugh at me. I want to call you Crisscross."

Nicco laughs out loud again, and I don't understand what is so funny.

"It can be a thing just between you and me, okay?" he says. "I'll call you"—he scratches his head—"Gabby. You call me"—he stops, and his forehead crinkles like he is thinking—"Cross. What do you think?"

I look up into his green eyes, and I smile.

"Nicknames just for us?"

"Yes, ma'am."

I smile big at him. He is so nice. I think we will be the bestest friends ever.

Cross's papa tells us that his mamma was in an accident, and she is with Jesus and the angels now. His mamma's parents came to live with them afterward to help. I look up at Cross, and when his papa talks about the angels, his lips quiver. He is sad. I would be sad, too, if my mamma went to live with the angels and did not come visit me. I will have to love him extra hard for her, so he is not sad anymore.

After dinner, the adults have yucky coffee while we all enjoy dessert that Cross's grandmother, Una, made. Then, they excuse themselves. Nicco looks to Cross and asks if he wants to ride bikes, and I ask if I can come, too.

"No, you can't even ride your bike without training wheels." He rolls his eyes.

I start to get upset because I want to go with them. I don't want to stay while the older boys play video games and the grown-ups talk in the study.

Why can't I go?

"Tell you what, Miss Gabby." Cross bends down and looks me in the eye. "Next time I come over, I will help you learn how to ride without training wheels. Then, you can always go with us. Deal?"

"Okay," I say through my tears.

He wraps one of my curls in his finger and tugs. "Don't cry. We will have lots of time to spend together now that we live just down the street. I promise."

"Cross your heart?"

"Cross my heart." He slashes his fingers over his heart and winks at me as he follows Nicco out the back door.

I think he might be my prince, just like Cinderella. Prince Cross.

CHAPTER
One

Brie
Present

A S I STEP OFF THE PLANE INTO THE HUSTLE AND BUSTLE OF LAX
Airport, anxiety kicks in. This is real. I'm doing this. I left
everything and everyone behind to begin again three thousand
miles away from home.

I follow the horde of rushing travelers through the packed airport and into a surprisingly empty restroom. I look in the mirror at the
weary face staring back at me. My chestnut eyes are slightly bloodshot,
and my long, dark locks are a tangled mess from sleeping over half the
flight from JFK. I splash some cool water on my face and run my fingers through my unruly hair. I pinch my cheeks and add a quick swipe
of gloss across my lips. I take one last moment to gather myself. It's as
ready as I am going to get.

I give myself a pep talk as I walk down to baggage claim to collect
my luggage. "You can do this. You are Brie Masters. You are a single girl
from the big city, here to experience life outside of your hometown bubble while finishing your degree." I work hard to convince myself as I
grab my bags from the belt and head out into the warm California sun.

I take a deep breath to calm myself. Calm is something I haven't
felt in a very long time. I'm not exactly sure what Los Angeles has to
offer a broken soul like me, but it has to be better than what I walked

away from. It just has to be. Starting over is not something I thought I would be doing at twenty-two years old, but here I am. I have lived a thousand lifetimes in those twenty-two years, and I have cried over the past long enough. Time to chase—and hopefully catch—a few new dreams. So, I gather myself and walk into my future.

"Jeez, Brie, how did you manage to pack your life into two suitcases? I don't think I have ever known a girl to travel on vacation this light, much less move across the country."

With an emphasis on the name I now choose to be called, my cousin, Daniel, ribs me as he lifts all the belongings I cared to carry with me into this new adventure into the bed of his pickup truck.

"I told you, I'm taking this moving-on thing very seriously. New everything. New name. New home. New friends. Even new clothes."

So far, I'm happy with my decision to move west and reconnect with my cousin. We were great friends when we were children—before his parents divorced, and he moved to Cali with his dad, Matthew Taylor. Uncle Matt had done well for himself as the premier Dentist to the Stars. I assume well-maintained teeth are a fairly lucrative commodity in Hollywood. Every single face aspiring to be on stage, screen, or print has to have them after all.

Daniel and I kept in touch through the years as much as possible. Sending each other birthday cards every year and placing the occasional telephone call when we were younger and seeing each other when he came to visit his mom, my mother's older sister, in the summers. Once we were old enough for social media accounts though, it was like he had never left. That is the thing about sites like Instagram and Twitter; you feel like you are actively participating in the lives of people you haven't set your eyes on in ten or more years. It is the best and the worst thing about social media. Disconnected connection.

It felt good to be in the same space as him now. He has grown into a handsome man, tall and broad-shouldered, like his dad. His dark hair is a little wild, and he still has the scar that runs through his left eyebrow from when he fell from the tire swing in my backyard when we were about six years old. He is sporting a five-o'clock shadow; actually, it looks more like a seven-o'clock shadow at this point. And, of course, he has a smile that could blind you, courtesy of his dad. He is all grown up and an aspiring musician, still living at home in his dad's pool house in Beverly Hills while he lives his dream. He is a talented guitar player and singer-songwriter. I just know he is going to be famous one day. I wanted freedom and a fresh start, but I longed for a familiar face that wasn't vetted to the past in a way that it would keep popping up on me. Daniel is that face.

"You have certainly come to the right place. A lot of miles between here and New York. They are two completely different worlds, but don't worry; I am sure you are going to fit right in. Dawn and Kelsey have already gotten your room ready, and they are excited to officially meet you."

Dawn Martin is Daniel's current girlfriend and his stepsister, Kelsey Green's, best friend and roommate. Uncle Matt married Kelsey's mom when Daniel and Kelsey were already temperamental teenagers, so their relationship was strained from the beginning. Her mom was a former dental client and a wilting flower of an actress who had found fame in the early nineties, playing the sexy villain on a popular network soap opera. Daniel didn't take too well to the two female drama queens coming into and taking over his and his dad's easy bachelor lives. However, once he started dating his new sister's best friend, much to her chagrin, they were forced into a tentative truce. According to Daniel though, they grew on each other and settled into a love/hate, familial relationship.

The girls' former roommate, Tonya, just vacated her room and moved out on her own. That left them with a room for rent and hopefully room in their inner circle for me. I could use some friends.

Daniel told me all about the two—the good, bad, and ugly—and I feel like I already know them. My favorite part about them is the ugly. I know that sounds insane, but maybe my ugly won't seem so bad next to theirs. I guess we all carry a bit of it with us, but I'm here to try to shed mine for good.

We pull up to a gorgeous stucco building in Santa Monica about thirty minutes later. It is a well-maintained place with a quaint courtyard and gated parking. It is close to the beach and the Third Street Promenade and definitely something I would never have been able to afford on my own, but with my savings and the money Una tucked into my hand as I left, I should, hopefully, be able to cover one-third of the cost until I can find a decent-paying job.

Enrolling in classes is my first order of business though. I graduated high school a few months early and then took time off to spend a couple of years in Paris with my mom's younger sister, Aunt Mitzi. It was a glorious time in my life. Paris is a dream, and Aunt Mitzi is one of my favorite people on the planet. She took a heartbroken teen in and showed her a whole new world full of culture, food, fashion, and excitement that only Paris could provide.

I started taking classes at NYU the semester following my return to New York, but a little more than a year in was when everything in my life went sideways. Looking back, I probably should have stayed in France and gone to university. I loved it there, but something—or better yet, someone—kept calling me back home. Him. No, he is not allowed here. No thoughts of him in my new life.

Daniel parks the truck and hops out. I gather my purse and phone and open the door. A wonderful aroma of salt and sea envelops me, and I instantly love it here. Fresh air. Fresh start.

"Apartment number is three-B, and the girls are waiting for you.

Go on up and say hi, and I'll grab your things and be up in a minute," Daniel instructs me as he types away on his phone.

I turn toward the courtyard and take it in. The space is a good size with a few large shade trees sprinkled about. There are cobblestone sidewalks lined with flower beds bursting with purple salvia and bright yellow coreopsis along the path. A couple of people are seated on benches under the trees, reading or typing away on their laptops, and one girl is lying on a beach towel, soaking up a few late rays of sunshine. *Yes, I will definitely love it here.*

I make my way to the center building and climb the exterior staircase leading up to the third floor. It is insane how anxious I am to meet my new roommates. *Will they be able to tell by looking at me the hell I have been through this past year? Is my outside as tattered as my inside?* I know these are silly thoughts because my scars don't show on the outside. They are not physical scars, not all of them anyway.

I reach the third floor, and I see 3B right at the top of the stairs. A shadow is peeking out of the front window before my foot even hits the landing, so I assume Daniel texted to let them know we had arrived. As I raise my knuckles to knock, the door swings open, and a tall, slender girl my age with shoulder-length blonde hair that has bright pink tips comes barreling for me and wraps her arms around me.

Dawn, I think to myself. *This must be Dawn.*

"Brie, we are so glad you are finally here," she practically squeals.

She smells like coconut, and I allow myself to absorb some of her enthusiasm as I squeeze her back and look behind her into my new home. It's intimidating, but she hooks her arm in mine and leads me in like we have known each other for ages.

"We have your room all ready for you. The bed is made up with fresh linens, and it has been thoroughly cleaned. Tonya took everything with her that wasn't nailed down, but all of the furniture is still here, so we'll just have to go shopping to get you all the essentials, like pillows, blankets, and a lamp. Not that you need too many blankets here. It's always warm."

She is talking a mile a minute as she leads me through the apartment, past a nice-sized living space and down a hall. I instantly like her.

"This is your room. It's the smallest of the three, but it has the best view. The ocean is across the street and down a couple of blocks. You have your own bathroom—well, sort of. It is the one across the hall, and it is also the guest bathroom when we have company. Kelsey and I have a Jack and Jill bath between our rooms, and we share it. Come on; I will show you the rest."

I follow her and check out both their rooms and the large-closet-sized space they use as a makeshift office with a tiny desk and shared computer and printer.

"Now, we come to our favorite spot in the entire apartment," she informs me as we round the living room.

She swings her arms wide in a dramatic game-show-hostess fashion. "Ta-da. The kitchen. This is where all the magic happens. We don't have a table or anything, but this island is massive, and the barstools are very comfy. It is the reason we rented this place. It is just so big and open. We like to cook, and we absolutely love to eat. There is a small deck through those sliding glass doors. It has an outdoor table and umbrella with a matching couch and electric fire pit. We sometimes like to sit out there and have coffee in the morning or dinner if it is a nice, cool evening. Or wine. We like our wine almost as much as we like our food."

She laughs, and I can't help but smile with her.

Kelsey, a petite girl with long blonde hair, is behind the island, cutting up what looks like bleu cheese and adding it to a board with other varieties, grapes, and crackers. My stomach growls at the sight.

"Yes, we do. We aren't exactly winos, but let's just say, we do our part to keep Napa Valley thriving." She looks up and adds, "Wow, look at you. You look like some exotic creature with your dark hair and olive skin. We don't see many Italian beauties around here. It's all bleached-blonde Valley girls with spray tans and fake tits. Present company excluded, of course." She slides her eyes to Dawn, who obviously has enhanced assets.

Dawn playfully sticks her tongue out at her friend. I can't help but notice that Kelsey is a natural stunner. Makeup free with a smattering of freckles across her nose. Her long hair is pulled back into a ponytail, and she is dressed in yoga pants and a tight tee.

I wonder if every girl in LA really is blonde and beautiful. It's very different from home. New York is a melting pot of ethnicity and culture, and everyone always seems to be made up to the max and in a hurry to be somewhere.

"I have some snacks here because we assumed you would be peckish after that long flight. We figured we would just call out for dinner later tonight after you had time to get settled in."

We hear Daniel enter the kitchen as I thank them for the warm welcome.

"No problem. We are happy to have someone new in here. Tonya was … well, she was …"

"She was the devil," Daniel finishes Kelsey's thought from the doorway.

Dawn walks over to him for a quick kiss and then admits, "Yeah, she was. I don't want you to think we are difficult to live with or anything. She was just in a bad mood most of the time and a bit on the lazy side. I mean, really, you are a twenty-three-year-old adult; wash your own dishes and pick your own clothes up off of the bathroom floor every once in a while." She rolls her eyes. "When she started hitting on Kelsey's boyfriend right in front of us one night, it was the straw that broke the camel's back. Girl Code. You never, ever break Girl Code. She had to go."

I get it. I have four brothers. *Tidy* is not a word in their vocabulary, and it drove me and my mother nuts. And I, too, have felt the sharp sting of a friend's betrayal.

"You guys don't have to worry about me. I like a clean and neat environment, too, and I have zero time or desire to hit on anyone at all. I'm focusing on me right now. Only me."

A look of relief passes between my new roomies, and I know—I just know—I am home.

other books

About
the author

Amber Kelly is a romance author that calls North Carolina home. She has been a avid reader from a young age and you could always find her with her nose in a book completely enthralled in an adventure. With the support of her husband and family, in 2018, she decided to finally give a voice to the stories in her head and her debut novel, Both of Me was born. You can connect with Amber on Facebook at facebook. com/AuthorAmberKelly, on IG @authoramberkelly, on twitter @ AuthorAmberKel1 or via her website www.authoramberkelly.com.

Made in the USA
Monee, IL
12 September 2024

65610964R00173